PYGMALION REVISITED

Cover art licensed from Shutterstock.com
Interior images licensed from Shutterstock.com

First print edition
ISBN 978-1-939275-62-2

DEDICATION
To those for whom love is an art and art is love.

Visit www.DevonLayne.com for information on new books and stories made available regularly.

Support the author via www.Patreon.com/aroslav Enjoy this work. Share it with friends! Write a review.

Pygmalion Revisited

Devon Layne

ELDER ROAD BOOKS
BELLEVUE WA

PREFACE

THIS PREFACE about the myth may be critical to your understanding of the stories in the cycle of *Pygmalion Revisited*.

Each chapter is an independent short story with a common theme. The stories run between 4,000 and 20,000 words. They all revolve around the love between an artist and his or her artwork. Each is a romantic story that involves one or more sexual episode. In some, the sex is limited but very sensual.

Many authors have riffed on the story of Pygmalion. The most famous in the English language is probably George Bernard Shaw's play Pygmalion on which the popular musical My Fair Lady was based. This is an example of the story with both a happy and a bittersweet ending. In Shaw's version, Eliza Doolittle leaves Henry Higgins and makes her own way in society, marrying Freddy Sanford-Hill, and opening a flower shop. Shaw held that Galatea, the sculpture embodied in Eliza, could only be truly considered alive if she were independent of the sculptor, Henry. In the musical, she returns to Henry and fetches his slippers. Well, we all want a happy ending. Each means something a little different.

You should have a passing familiarity with the story of Pygmalion. Our most dependable source for the story is from an epic poem by Ovid, titled *Metamorphoses*, that recites most of Greek and Latin mythology in a single narrative. Frankly, making sense of Ovid's poem might be challenging but I have included it below. To our contemporary ears, the language is certainly stilted at best.

The very short version:

PYGMALION IS A sculptor on the island of Cyprus, probably sometime in the third or fourth century B.C. He has become disgusted with the behavior of the priestesses of Aphrodite (the Propoetides) who have turned their back on the goddess and have become common prostitutes, selling their bodies in the name of love. Pygmalion himself is devoted to the goddess and swears off all women and refuses to take a wife.

He carves a statue from ivory. This is an obvious problem with the Ovid rendition, for it is a life-size statue and I have difficulty imagining any animal that could yield an ivory tusk or tooth that size. It probably means a piece of ivory-colored marble of which we have many examples in Hellenic and pre-Hellenic sculpture—some of which the English actually left in Greece. The statue is so lifelike and so beautiful that Pygmalion begins to treat it as if it were real, dressing it, putting jewelry on it, and even kissing and fondling it. He creates a bed for it and a soft pillow for its head.

At the festival of Aphrodite, Pygmalion brings his sacrifice and prays that the goddess might bring him a wife who is "the living likeness of my ivory girl." The sacrifice is accepted. When he gets back to his studio, he repeats his ritual of kissing and fondling his statue and discovers the lips warm and her breast pliable. She opens her eyes and he names her Galatea. They are married and have two children according to the story, the first ten months later. Aphrodite turns the unfaithful priestesses to stone.

And here is Ovid's version:

PYGMALION REVISITED

The Transformations of the Propoetides

The blasphemous Propoetides deny'd
Worship of Venus, and her pow'r defy'd:
But soon that pow'r they felt, the first that sold
Their lewd embraces to the world for gold.
Unknowing how to blush, and shameless grown,
A small transition changes them to stone.

The Story of Pygmalion and the Statue

Pygmalion loathing their lascivious life,
Abhorr'd all womankind, but most a wife:
So single chose to live, and shunn'd to wed,
Well pleas'd to want a consort of his bed.
Yet fearing idleness, the nurse of ill,
In sculpture exercis'd his happy skill;
And carv'd in iv'ry such a maid, so fair,
As Nature could not with his art compare,
Were she to work; but in her own defence
Must take her pattern here, and copy hence.
Pleas'd with his idol, he commends, admires,
Adores; and last, the thing ador'd, desires.
A very virgin in her face was seen,
And had she mov'd, a living maid had been:
One wou'd have thought she cou'd have stirr'd, but
strove
With modesty, and was asham'd to move.
Art hid with art, so well perform'd the cheat,
It caught the carver with his own deceit:
He knows 'tis madness, yet he must adore,
And still the more he knows it, loves the more:
The flesh, or what so seems, he touches oft,
Which feels so smooth, that he believes it soft.
Fir'd with this thought, at once he strain'd the breast,
And on the lips a burning kiss impress'd.

Devon Layne

'Tis true, the harden'd breast resists the gripe,
And the cold lips return a kiss unripe:
But when, retiring back, he look'd again,
To think it iv'ry, was a thought too mean:
So wou'd believe she kiss'd, and courting more,
Again embrac'd her naked body o'er;
And straining hard the statue, was afraid
His hands had made a dint, and hurt his maid:
Explor'd her limb by limb, and fear'd to find
So rude a gripe had left a livid mark behind:
With flatt'ry now he seeks her mind to move,
And now with gifts (the pow'rful bribes of love),
He furnishes her closet first; and fills
The crowded shelves with rarities of shells;
Adds orient pearls, which from the conchs he drew,
And all the sparkling stones of various hue:
And parrots, imitating human tongue,
And singing-birds in silver cages hung:
And ev'ry fragrant flow'r, and od'rous green,
Were sorted well, with lumps of amber laid between:
Rich fashionable robes her person deck,
Pendants her ears, and pearls adorn her neck:
Her taper'd fingers too with rings are grac'd,
And an embroider'd zone surrounds her slender waste.
Thus like a queen array'd, so richly dress'd,
Beauteous she shew'd, but naked shew'd the best.
Then, from the floor, he rais'd a royal bed,
With cov'rings of Sydonian purple spread:
The solemn rites perform'd, he calls her bride,
With blandishments invites her to his side;
And as she were with vital sense possess'd,
Her head did on a plumy pillow rest.

The feast of Venus came, a solemn day,

PYGMALION REVISITED

To which the Cypriots due devotion pay;
With gilded horns the milk-white heifers led,
Slaughter'd before the sacred altars, bled.

Pygmalion off'ring, first approach'd the shrine,
And then with pray'rs implor'd the Pow'rs divine:
Almighty Gods, if all we mortals want,
If all we can require, be yours to grant;
Make this fair statue mine, he wou'd have said,
But chang'd his words for shame; and only pray'd,
Give me the likeness of my iv'ry maid.

The golden Goddess, present at the pray'r,
Well knew he meant th' inanimated fair,
And gave the sign of granting his desire;
For thrice in chearful flames ascends the fire.
The youth, returning to his mistress, hies,
And impudent in hope, with ardent eyes,
And beating breast, by the dear statue lies.
He kisses her white lips, renews the bliss,
And looks, and thinks they redden at the kiss;
He thought them warm before: nor longer stays,
But next his hand on her hard bosom lays:
Hard as it was, beginning to relent,
It seem'd, the breast beneath his fingers bent;
He felt again, his fingers made a print;
'Twas flesh, but flesh so firm, it rose against the dint:
The pleasing task he fails not to renew;
Soft, and more soft at ev'ry touch it grew;
Like pliant wax, when chasing hands reduce
The former mass to form, and frame for use.
He would believe, but yet is still in pain,
And tries his argument of sense again,
Presses the pulse, and feels the leaping vein.

XI

Devon Layne

Convinc'd, o'erjoy'd, his studied thanks, and praise,
To her, who made the miracle, he pays:
Then lips to lips he join'd; now freed from fear,
He found the savour of the kiss sincere:
At this the waken'd image op'd her eyes,
And view'd at once the light, and lover with surprize.
The Goddess, present at the match she made,
So bless'd the bed, such fruitfulness convey'd,
That ere ten months had sharpen'd either horn,
To crown their bliss, a lovely boy was born;
Paphos his name, who grown to manhood, wall'd
The city Paphos, from the founder call'd.

PYGMALION REVISITED

What follows is my own romantic telling of the classical tale of "Pygmalion", trying to stick as close to the original intent as possible. The story is set in ancient Cyprus and I have done my best to be true to the culture and the time, but I live now, not then, so I made no attempt to stylize the language. It's contemporary.

I've used a few Greek terms that I've tried to make sure are adequately explained in the context. I should also note that the names of the tools the sculptor uses are Italian. Live with it. I couldn't find Greek equivalents of the Italian names used today.

So here goes. Enjoy!

PYGMALION

"EXCUSE ME Miss," Pygmalion said shyly. "Could you... Would you mind... I mean..."

"Aren't you a cutie, all tongue-tied?" The young woman answered. "What is it you want, handsome? Just say it. Anything you want."

"I was wondering if you would stand just a little more to the left so the light hits you better."

"Stand? You mean here? Like this?" She moved slightly and he nodded.

"Lift your head just a little." She did. Pygmalion quickly bent to his tablet and began scratching on it with charcoal. She was so beautiful. He worked quickly but carefully.

Seeing what he was doing, the young woman smiled. She canted her hips a little and thrust out her bosom. Then she took deep rhythmic breaths, lifting her breasts with each inhale and letting them fall as she exhaled. Pygmalion looked up at her and noticed her loose tunic gapped open slightly and from this angle he could see just a hint of color crowning the proud mound of her breast. He tore his eyes away from the sight and continued to draw. So smooth. So perfect. So inviting. In his drawing, he let the tunic fall open enough to see the aroused nipple as if showing through the thin fabric. Her bearing was regal. Her throat was long and exposed from her chin to the cleft between her breasts—thin and elegant. Her hair was caught back in ringlets, each tied to the one before it. Her arms were bare, the flawless skin exposed to the shoulder. Below her thin waist, her hips flared. He trailed his eyes downward

1

where she had subtly gathered her skirt in her hand to show her shapely leg. His eye involuntarily rose to her breast again. He was sure it was more fully exposed than it had been just a moment before. He glanced nervously around the agora, but no one seemed to notice him or the young woman brazenly showing herself to him on the temple steps. He used his thumb to blend the tones of her flesh as the perfectly shaped breast met her ribcage. He could almost feel her skin beneath his fingers. So sensuous.

"Are you finished yet?" Pygmalion realized he had stopped drawing, his thumb still caressing her nipple, barely touching the charcoal on the tablet.

"Yes. Thank you very much. Very much."

"That will be a silver penny."

"What?"

"For standing here in the heat posing while you drew. You need to tip me."

"Oh. Yes. Of course." Pygmalion fumbled in his purse, moving aside several pieces of charcoal in order to reach the coin. "Are you a professional?"

"Not full time. I have other duties, but men pay better."

"Well, thank you."

"Wait. What's your rush? Let me see the drawing."

"Um, okay." He held the tablet toward her, but she pushed him gently to the step and sat on his lap before pulling his hand around her to look at the drawing.

"Hmm. Not very good, are you?"

"What? It's a quick sketch. And besides, charcoal isn't truly my medium. Marble is. I just need reference material."

"Oh? You intend to carve my boob in stone? You seem to really like it."

"What?"

"Well, look how well-developed my boob is compared to my face. Just the hint of an eyebrow and a line for the lips. But the texture and shading of my boob is exquisite. Look." She held her tunic open just far enough that he could easily see down her front and her entire left breast. "See? It's so real and lifelike that you could almost reach out and touch it." He no longer knew if she was referring to the picture or to herself. His heart was beating more rapidly as he felt his manhood become turgid beneath her. "Would you like to?"

"Like to?"

"Like to reach out and touch it? Caress my skin. Feel how hard my nipple becomes beneath your hand?" She squirmed in his lap a little, bringing his penis to a full erection. "You must have a lot of stress in your job—trying to make sure it's all perfect, not daring to chip away the wrong thing. I could help you... uh, unblock your muse. Get your... creative juices flowing, so to speak. We could go just inside and find a private space where you could explore my various aspects to your heart's content. I'll teach you what a real woman feels like. You can even draw me again if you must. Let the function of clothing truly follow my form."

"I don't... where?"

"Just in the temple there."

"In the temple? What are you?"

"I'm a priestess. But what can I say? What does any man want from the goddess but to get laid? I'm in the business of answering prayers. For a modest fee, of course. Two silver for the room and a gold for me. Come and let me make you come." She reached between them to stroke his cock.

"I... but... that's prostitution! You are a priestess of the goddess."

"So, you think I should give it up for free? The goddess is a myth. I am real and I'm available."

"No! No. I am sorry." Pygmalion tried twice to stand before dislodging the prostitute priestess. She stood and straightened her robes.

"Sure? I promise I'll make it worth your time. That sudden release of inspiration would do you good," she said, reaching for him again.

"That's… it's an abomination! How could you sell your body in the name of the goddess?"

"All the priestesses do it. It's how the temple stays open, how we pay for our shelter and food."

He looked into her kohl-rimmed eyes, seeing past her friendliness and nearly retching at what he saw. So cleverly concealed behind a pleasing body and face, she was hard, mercenary, her intent on his purse rather than on him. There was no goddess here. No love. Nothing but a business transaction. He looked again at his drawing and then threw it at her feet as he ran from the public plaza.

PYGMALION WASSICK. Throwing-up-in-the-alley-like-an-all-night-drunk sick. And he'd had no wine. The day had started well. He took his tablet to the market square in front of the temple to look at people and draw. A concept had vaguely begun to take shape in his mind for a wonderful new sculpture for the prince's vestibule in praise of Aphrodite, but he needed to look at people more closely—how they stood when they spoke to each other, how they stood or sat when they thought no one was watching. Then she appeared on the temple steps and it was magnificent. He wanted to capture the sun shining through the fabric of her skirts, showing the shape of her legs. How could he capture that in marble?

But she was a prostitute. That in itself didn't bother him. Many women were prostitutes and, though some were worn and weary, many were happy enough. It was better than starving, one older woman told him.

But she was a priestess of Aphrodite! The Propoetides were sacred to Aphrodite. No man would dare touch them

4

inappropriately. And worse, she had called blessed Aphrodite a myth — set herself up to be able to answer prayers. Offered her body as a substitute for faith.

Pygmalion threw up again.

I will never look upon a woman again! They are a disgrace to the goddess.

"So you will tar all women with the disgrace of the Propoetides?" a voice said nearby.

What? Did I say that aloud?

Pygmalion looked around and saw an old man sitting on a step at the end of the alley. Both hands were on the knob of a crooked cane and his white beard nearly touched his lap. Yet his piercing blue eyes were clear and Pygmalion felt nailed to the spot beneath their gaze.

"I beg your pardon, sir? Did you speak to me?"

"Yes. You say women are a disgrace to the goddess. Are you ready to paint them all the same? Or should I say, 'Cut them from the same block of marble'?"

"How could one trust a woman once the Propoetides have forsaken the goddess and turned to prostitution? They are her own! They walk with the goddess each day and yet they call her a myth."

"Well, you don't have to trust them to enjoy them. Personally, I thank the goddess for every young woman who deigns to smile upon me. Anything else she does is worthy of making an offering."

"And so, you would defile a priestess, old man?"

"The priestess herself may be an answer to prayer. But you are an artist. What natural form is more perfect than the shape of a woman? When the white marble comes down from the mountains and you stand looking at those shapeless blocks, what do you first see? The very color and texture of the stone cry out, 'Here is a woman!' When you touch her cold surface, you feel not the stone, but the perfect shape beneath it."

"A woman carved of stone is pure and undefiled. A woman in the flesh is… I have no words. I must go home."

"Feeling better now? Nothing to settle your stomach like the thought of cold hard marble."

Pygmalion turned to snap at the old man, but no one was there.

THE SHAPE WAS perfect and Pygmalion switched from the *gradina* chisel to the *scalpello*. He worked steadily, the rhythm of his mallet on the chisel even and sure. This block was not large because Pygmalion did not want to waste material on his great experiment. He would be laughed at, surely, but it was a perfect form. Even the streak of blue that cut through the almost pristine cream-colored marble made a statement. Perfection was flawed. There was nothing perfect in the world.

For days, he worked in his studio, keeping the work hidden from prying eyes. The second piece of the sculpture had to be even more exactingly carved. It must match as a perfect inverse of the first. They had to fit together without a hair's breadth between them. It would be dramatic then when the first piece began to float and then to spin.

"I MUST HAVE the exact weight of the *bala*," Demetrius complained. "And I need to know when I can work on the *lekani* to plumb it. Why did you make it so big?"

"Big? I thought it was small. No one will see it or understand unless they are standing right next to it. It is scarcely a sculpture to decorate the agora with," Pygmalion argued.

"But for the entryway of the *palati*?"

"Yes. If our patron is pleased, it will reside in the center of the *prothalamos*. But who will see it there? It is not as if most people walk in the front door of the Prince's home."

"No. Only rich people who can afford to commission a sculpture from you." They laughed and then set about the serious work of weighing and measuring the sculpture. Demetrius had devised a piston driven pump that would create the right amount of water pressure and began the task of plumbing the basin. Pygmalion stroked the sculpture with his hands searching for any imperfection in the surface.

Cold hard stone. How wrong the old man was. The stone was pliable beneath the touch of his chisel and rasp. He could feel the heartbeat within it and the warmth of its life.

"I AM READY," Agathos declared. "Let us see this new creation."

Pygmalion stepped forward and released a cord that held the drape in front of his sculpture. There was silence as the small crowd looked first at the sculpture and then at their prince. The prince approached the ball sitting in a basin on a pedestal. He walked around it. He stood back and studied it. Finally, he spoke.

"Where are her boobs?"

There was shocked silence before the prince broke into laughter.

"Who was the model?" laughed his wife. "My shape is certainly nothing like that."

"Not at all!" the prince declared, hefting his wife's bosom before the people gathered.

"My Lord," Pygmalion said. "If I may." He felt the throb of the pump from beneath his feet and stretched a hand out to the sphere. They had tested it, of course, but that had been in the studio. If the pressure was too little, nothing would happen. Pygmalion touched the basin and felt moisture gathered around the edge. He touched the ball and gave it a gentle push. Had the ball been all white, no one would have noticed its movement. But the streak of blue that cut through the marble moved, rose and fell as the globe spun in its socket, lubricated by the water. There were noises of amazement and the prince fell back a step.

"Is this magic that the marble changes its stripe?" the prince asked.

"It may look magical," Pygmalion answered, "but the ball is floating on water and is slowly rotating."

"But how does if float? It is a stone. Stone's sink."

There was a brief argument and explanation and the prince was finally satisfied once he was taken to the cavern beneath the floor where Demetrius' ingenious pump was working. At last, the prince, his wife, and his guests were satisfied and returned to the vestibule to stare at the slowly rotating ball of marble.

"You are a prince among sculptors, Pygmalion. You shall be richly rewarded… after I receive the sculptures that I want. I want beautiful women. A garden full of them. You got away with putting this… interesting form in my entry. Well, my guests will not expect that. But in my garden, I want women. Lovely, perfect, naked women. When you deliver them, you will have a kingdom of your own. Until then, nothing."

"My Lord, Prince Agathos, I have foresworn women. I shall neither touch them nor carve them. I find women… disappointing."

"Then you haven't known the women I have known. But no matter what your preferences, I do not want a garden full of little boys."

"No, my Lord. That is not what I mean."

"It makes no difference to me. Little boys can be a comfort when a man is between women. But I will have a garden full of exquisite women carved in that ivory stone you like so much before you have a silver penny for your sculpture."

Pygmalion Revisited

PYGMALION WEPT.

He lay on his cot in the chamber next to his studio, head buried against his arms, and cried out to his goddess. It was not a cry of words but his heart rending in her presence. He had been so sure that the cleverness of his spherical sculpture would win the prince. The prince was pleased enough, but refused to pay unless Pygmalion forsook his vow and sculpted a woman. How could he do this?

"It might have been better if you'd floated a cube instead of a sphere."

Pygmalion spun in his bed at the sound, sending tears flying. On the chair beside his bed sat a woman. No. So much more than a woman. A goddess. With that realization, Pygmalion rolled from his bed and prostrated himself on the floor.

"My Goddess," he whispered.

"Rise, Pygmalion. You've pleased me."

He looked up, startled. Pleased Aphrodite? When? How?

"Not like that!" the goddess laughed. "Yet. It pleases me that you see my priestesses for the whores they have become and that you have forsaken the company of women for my honor. You are true to me."

"May I never forsake my vows to you, Precious Goddess." He began to prostrate himself again, but a hand on his arm pulled him up. The goddess gently pushed him back to sit on his cot.

"Yes. I honor your devotion. But if your goddess asked you to do something, then that would not be against your vows since you have made your vow to your goddess, no?" Pygmalion tried to parse her words. His vow was to the goddess and therefore he would not be in violation of it if he were following her instructions.

"Can you possibly want me to fulfill the commission of the prince?" Pygmalion asked.

"I take vows quite seriously, Pygmalion. That is why I am upset over the same things that you are."

9

"The Propoetides."

"They vowed to serve me. Granted, I am a goddess of love and such service could include acts of love."

"But it is not that they have sex with devotees," Pygmalion rushed in. "I have been with a priestess," he said, blushing. "But that was before. When I lay with her, I felt your presence and your blessing. Now... they don't believe. They don't even blush at their actions. I wish *they* were stone statues."

Aphrodite stared at the sculptor, a smile slowly creeping across her lips. She forestalled his question.

"For now, we must get you working on Agathos' commission."

"But I cannot sculpt a woman."

"Look at me, Pygmalion." As he looked at her, the goddess stood and let her robes fall to the ground. Pygmalion's mouth opened and his hands clasped over his lap so the goddess would not be offended by his manly response. His eyes fell first to her bosom and involuntarily trailed down to her sex before he tore them away to look at her eyes. "It is acceptable, Pygmalion. If I did not want you to look, I would not have commanded it. Look. Look at all of me." As she spoke, she slowly turned so Pygmalion could see the proud thrust of her breasts in profile and then the fullness of her bottom, round and sensuous. He could see her cleft as she continued to turn toward him and could almost catch her scent. "Am I beautiful, Pygmalion?"

Pygmalion knew that his goddess, for all her good traits, was vain. It had been shown many times before. He would be a fool to say anything but yes, but even if it was not for the fear of her wrath, what he saw filled him with such intense desire that he could not have answered otherwise.

"The judgment of Paris stands, my Goddess," he breathed. "Please let me bow and worship you."

"Well, that didn't work out so well. But Paris and Helen are centuries turned to dust. Let us see if we can do better by you."

She held out her hand to Pygmalion and he touched her for the first time. "Come to me, Pygmalion. The worship I crave cannot be done when you are bowed." He stood before his goddess and realized that she was not quite as tall as he thought. She lifted her lips to him and he kissed her.

His heart stopped. He kissed the goddess Aphrodite— Astarte of old—the goddess of the spring ritual—the goddess of love, beauty, pleasure, and... procreation. He kissed her and surely now he must die. He was content.

"Are my lips soft, my artist? Do you feel the hardness of my nipples when I press against your chest? Do your hands find any flaw when they caress my skin, my back, my buttocks? Do not pass from me, my love. Touch me. Part the folds of my sex and feel the moisture. Place your lips on my nipple and suckle me like a newborn. Worship my body with your hands, your lips, your tongue, your cock. Enter me and know that I am your goddess and you are my love."

Pygmalion's heart restarted as his throbbing cock released his seed in the depths of the goddess and she moaned against his shoulder as they stood linked together.

"Now," she whispered when their breathing slowed and they sat on his cot, still holding each other, "we must find a way to let you fulfill your commission without breaking your vow. You, my lover, my friend, my artist, will carve your statue—not of a woman, but of a goddess. I will model for you and you will release me from the stone."

"Yes, my goddess," he whispered. "I will do whatever you command."

"That is what I love about you."

"HOW MANY BLOCKS of marble?" asked the astounded *kyrios*.

"His Highness' command was 'a garden full of naked women.' You know the palace better than I. Exactly how many naked women does a 'garden full' comprise?" Pygmalion asked the chief of the prince's staff as they walked between huge blocks of marble.

"Very well. Thirteen. Twelve for the garden and one to replace what you ruin."

I will not ruin one.

"Humor him, my love."

"Goddess?"

"Who are you talking to?" the *kyrios* demanded. Pygmalion looked around, but saw no one else near.

"He can neither hear nor see me," a voice whispered in his ear. "I have reserved that for you."

"I am honored."

"Indeed, you are," the major domo snorted. "He could have had Mathias sculpt his gallery. The cost would be much lower."

"The cost would not be the only thing lower. Even his statues have warts."

"So, he could just chisel them off. It's only stone."

"My dear Kyrios, I believe you have as low an opinion of art as I have of women."

"Besides, Mathias only does busts," the goddess laughed. "I think he was weaned too soon." Pygmalion snorted and the chief of staff glared at him.

"Be that as it may, you can go and I'll have the stone delivered to your studio."

"Oh no. I shall choose each block. They must be perfect."

"I chose the block for your vestibule sculpture and instead of following the prince's instructions, you made a mechanical contraption."

"Exactly. What would the prince think of the statue of a beautiful woman with a blue streak running across her breasts? I did the best thing possible with the travesty of material you supplied. This time I will choose my own stones and they will be the finest ivory white marble of Thassos."

"You will make a white goddess that is flawless, my love," whispered the goddess as she tugged his arm toward the blocks to be considered.

"Thassos! That is the most expensive..." the *kyrios* said to his back as the sculptor appeared to be dragged away. Shaking his head the *kyrios* found the stone master and instructed him to bill thirteen blocks of marble that Pygmalion would choose to the prince's domicile.

Pygmalion walked up to the first block in the row of new deliveries from Greece. He laid his hands on the stone and thought. He couldn't see the figure within. The goddess laughed.

"Not that one; it's dead," the goddess said. "How about this one?" she asked approaching a block some fifteen feet tall. Pygmalion watched as the goddess shed her clothes and walked into the stone, turning in various poses, making the stone transparent for Pygmalion to see what would result. "Does this marble make my ass look big?" Aphrodite asked. It made everything look big, but Pygmalion was not about to say that.

"I believe we want something that is life-size," he said cautiously. "This block is fit for a temple, but not for a simple prince's *peristyle*."

"There is no block here large enough for a life-size statue of me," the goddess said smugly. "I suppose, though that we need human life-size and not goddess-size. Let's try this one." She stepped out of the mammoth block and into a block that was nearer the size that would be needed. She controlled her size and posed in the block.

"That's very nice. I like that one," Pygmalion said as he approached the stone. He placed his hand on the surface, but could feel the shape of the goddess beneath his fingertips. He caressed her softly.

"If you continue that, we will attract a crowd as you hump a block of marble," she whispered. It was obvious to Pygmalion that he was not the only one aroused. He backed away from the block and took the goddess' hand as she stepped down.

Pygmalion noticed that she did not bother to clothe herself again as she moved from one stone block to another, posing and primping in each. In each block, Pygmalion could see a different pose. There would be no row of near-identical *Korai* standing at attention here. Each stone would be a unique woman in her own pose. None of the poses the goddess struck were exactly lewd, but she kept no secrets hidden. At last they had chosen twelve blocks that pleased them both.

"They are all wonderful and what minor flaws there are in the stone I can remove as I carve, but I know none of these are the sculpture you want me to carve. We are running out of choices," Pygmalion whispered so no one would overhear him talking to a goddess whose nude body was wrapped around him but invisible to all others.

"Yes. Those are for the prince and his cronies to gawk at and fantasize about. They will be real enough that even his wife will be jealous of the attention he pays them. But now we need the one stone that will be ours and ours alone. It will be the stone from which you render your lover."

"My goddess, you know that my simple skill will never capture your true beauty nor the depth of passion I feel for you. When I touch the cold surface, I can feel your presence, but no other would ever recognize you in the depths of stone."

"You will create the perfect woman, my artist. When you touch her, you will feel me respond." They were deep in the stone market when they came upon a block covered with canvas. Pygmalion pulled the cloth from the stone gently, as if taking the clothes from his lover. Beneath was the purest white marble he had ever seen.

"It is like ivory, it is so pure," he breathed. The cover had kept dust from collecting in the cutting grooves. Even these showed no impurities. It was the finest block of marble he had ever seen.

"No. No. You may not have that!" exclaimed a man rushing down the narrow aisle of stones. "That block must be..." He stuttered to a halt before them and knelt before them, much to Pygmalion's confusion. "My goddess," the man uttered. *He can see her?*

"You are not the only true believer, Pygmalion. Thanos, you have done well and shall be richly rewarded," Aphrodite said to the stone merchant. Pygmalion noticed that she was clothed again and that assuaged his momentary jealousy. "Please deliver this stone and the others Pygmalion has marked to his studio. And charge the prince double what he would normally pay," the goddess said.

"My goddess, for you I would charge nothing. Yet I will do as you command."

"You have always been a faithful servant. I will speak with you soon about more stone and where it will be delivered. I want to improve the temple at my birthplace."

"Thank you, Goddess. Pygmalion, I am honored to provide this ivory marble to you. Cut well."

SEVERAL DAYS PASSED after the marble blocks had been delivered. They were scattered through the studio as though he would work on all of them at once. Yet, in the center sat the ivory marble the goddess had taken residence in. For hours, Pygmalion sat in front of the stone, beside the stone, behind the stone, holding the stone in his arms. Occasionally, he would reach for charcoal and sketch a line on its surface. Most of the time, he simply sat with his fingers moving softly against the stone's surface.

"Are you teasing me, my love?" Aphrodite asked from the depths of the stone. "Time means nothing to me, but you should begin your work before you are too old to lift a hammer." Pygmalion sighed.

"My goddess, fear stays my hand. You have asked me to create the perfect woman and have offered yourself as my model. What if my hand slips or my poor skill insults your deity? Perhaps I should practice on one of the lesser stones."

"Pygmalion, are you committed to me?" she asked softly. He felt her hand caress his face.

"Yes, oh yes."

"Then commit to the stone. Free me. Find me here in the depths of this perfect ivory and release me."

Pygmalion picked up his *scapezzatore* and *mazza*. With a slow stroke he began the pitching. The first chips flew before him and soon he had picked up a rhythm. Occasionally, he set aside the chisel and mallet and sketched lines on the stone with his charcoal. Again, he picked up the tools and lost himself in the rhythms.

By the third day, he switched to the *subbia*, and began shaping the reclining goddess within. This process was much slower than the pitching. His mallet continued the constant rhythmic tapping, but much smaller pieces were removed with each tap. As the form emerged, Pygmalion spent more and more time touching the shape with his hands, listening to the soft moans of the goddess within as he touched her flesh of stone.

He began working with the *unghietto*, the little fingernail, as he smoothed the surface of her face and cut individual strands of hair on her head. The rasp shaped the contours of her face and nose. He changed to an emery stone as he smoothed her luscious, parted lips.

"How kind of you to shape my face first. I thought perhaps you would go directly for my boobs. Isn't that what the little slut at the temple accused you of?" the stone whispered to him. He moistened a cloth and wiped the dust from her face and eyes, half-lidded with lust. He dampened her lips with the swab and then bent to softly kiss them. She sighed.

"I love your breasts, Goddess. I love the texture of your skin and the heat of your sex. But I would sacrifice all for the taste of your lips."

"When you finish the carving, you will have them all."

He petted her hair and looked at the position of her head. He jerked back.

"One moment, Goddess." He ran from the studio to his apartment and snatched up a pillow. "Here. I did not mean to put you in a position where you would have to hold your head up while I work. This pillow will cushion you."

"Pygmalion, I am made of stone. Is it not strong enough to hold my head in position?"

"Yes, Goddess, but humor me. I would not have you in discomfort because I did not think of a resting place for your head."

"I love you, my artist. And I thank you for your concern. I feel that my time with you is fading, even as you progress on my sculpture. When it is finished, I will no longer be with you in this way. So, take your time. Even in a form such as this, your caress enflames my heart."

TIME AND WORK progressed. As he worked, he talked to the goddess and told her his dreams. Had he not become disillusioned, he had hoped to marry one day and have children. He hoped even yet to please his patron and occasionally worried about the untouched blocks of marble that still awaited his chisel. Through all this, Aphrodite comforted him and filled his senses with her touch, even as he gently formed her shoulders and her bosom.

He began to shape a cloth draped across her for modesty but she stopped that thought at once.

"Do not cover me, lover," she said. "No eyes will caress my shape but yours. Let me show myself fully to you."

Fully, included carefully smoothing the tender rise of her breasts, the slight puffiness of her areolae with the nipples rising proudly from their centers. He kissed her lips as he caressed the supple breasts. He bent to suck her marble nipples. Though he knew they were just ivory stone, he could almost taste the mother's milk that would fill them when she suckled a child.

Voices interrupted his revelry and he pulled a blanket over the sculpture so her nakedness could not be seen.

"Look. He is so modest he even covers the statue's privates."

"That is so we won't see his semen covering her stony stomach," laughed another.

"Dear Pygmalion, wouldn't you rather a flesh-and-blood woman to sink your throbbing manhood into? I volunteer my flesh and blood — for a price," coaxed a third.

The twelve chattering women filled his studio, some tugging at the blanket and some tugging at him. The daughters of Propoetus had come to mock him and tempt him from his well-known vow.

"You need to have a model, Pygmalion," said one. She shed her tunic and pulled his hand to her breast. "How does this compare, artist? Squeeze. Does it not feel better than cold, hard stone?"

"Touch *me*," said another of the suddenly naked women. She dragged his fingers through her slit. "I am wet and hot. Think how this would feel to your hard cock as I slid up and down on your rigid pole." Pygmalion snatched his hands back and grabbed to prevent the blanket from being dislodged.

"Look sisters!" said one as she posed naked in front of a block of uncut stone. "I'm a statue. Perhaps if we model for him he will pay as much attention to us as he does to his imaginary friend there." Each of the sisters posed in front of a block of white marble, heads thrown back as if I ecstasy, breasts cupped and offered to the viewer, legs parted as they reclined to take a lover. As he looked at them, he could see the stone take shape in his mind's eye.

"Your hearts are already made of stone and your breasts colder than granite," Pygmalion declared. "Go! Live your wanton lives while you still can. The goddess will visit her retribution on you. You will have eternity to rue your rejection of her."

"You've been brainwashed," the eldest said. "The goddess is a myth—no more a woman than the stone you shape with your hands."

"Who could believe in a goddess born as a teenager, rising from the sea on a shell in all her naked beauty to seduce both gods and men?" The women had begun to close in a circle around him.

"It is a myth created by ugly men who would have the most beautiful woman married to the crippled and deformed Hephaestus. A fairy tale to dream on when he could simply pay a gold coin and have a true beauty take him between her thighs."

"Even you, Pygmalion, hardened by the hammer and chisel, could be gentled within my sex."

"Give up your vow, sculptor. Come to my bed and bring a gold coin for your pleasure."

"Bring twelve gold coins and you shall have a night with each of us."

"Go, I said! You are an abomination. There will be no hope for you when the goddess takes her revenge."

The women laughed and abruptly turned to gather their clothes. They dressed sloppily and laughed as they filed out of the studio, helping each other tie their straps.

"I am so sorry, goddess," Pygmalion wept as he cast himself on the marble form.

"Hush, my love. You still have company."

Pygmalion turned to see the youngest of the Propoetides still in the studio leaning against and stroking one of the blocks of stone. He straightened himself and approached the young woman who had attempted to seduce him at the temple just months ago. She turned toward him.

"I can see myself," she whispered. "I can see myself in the stone. Will you carve me, Pygmalion? Will you make me immortal?"

"Would you truly wish to share in your sisters' fate? It is not too late, but the goddess will not wait forever."

"You frighten me, Pygmalion. Everyone knows... My sisters taught me..." A tear trickled down her face. "I am what I am. How I wish I were a virgin again and could offer myself to you, new and pristine and filled with your faith. But I am what I am."

"Sephane! Come! We have business at the temple waiting. Fun time is over," called one of the sisters from outside. The priestess reached to Pygmalion's cheek and touched him softly before she turned and ran from the studio.

"That was sad," Aphrodite whispered in his ear. He was still standing by the stone, seeing the young priestess in it as she had herself. The goddess stood next to him, not encased in the statue he was carving.

"Can anything be done?" he asked.

"She is the only one that can save her," the goddess answered. "Come, my love. We have little time left until your masterpiece is finished. Come make love to me and worship my body and spirit." Instead of returning to the stone, the couple retired to Pygmalion's apartment where the goddess of love showed him all her art and accepted his worship.

"YOU'RE TICKLING," THE goddess giggled as Pygmalion ran the emery around her toes. "Does this mean that I am finished?" she asked sadly.

"Not quite, my love. I am going to bathe you."

"Bathe me?"

"In pumice first. Then when I am satisfied that there is not a single blemish on your skin, I will polish you with tin oxide. By this time tomorrow you will positively glow."

"And that will be just in time for me to make it to the temple for the festival. I am sad, lover, though I knew this would not last forever. You are, after all, mortal. It would be selfish of me to monopolize you. And there will be some who come with genuine sacrifices during the festival and I will honor them as I honor you. You have made me look more kindly upon men. Most believe they know best and ignore my urging."

"You mean Adonis?"

"Tell a man not to do something and he immediately goes out and does it. That did it for fucking Ares, though. He is completely cut off."

BEFORE THE FINAL polish, Pygmalion brought a colorful blanket on which to lay the statue. He placed pearls around her neck and a new pillow beneath her head. As he worked the polish into her breasts he felt arousal take the goddess. He spent extra time polishing her nipples until they shone.

"I will miss you, Goddess," he said as he moved down her stomach with the polish. The moisture he felt was not entirely that of the polish he applied.

"And I will miss you. Oh! That feels good. Polish that a little more and kiss me, love. Yes. Just a little more."

Pygmalion felt her convulse in her climax, the moisture on his fingers pulsing. Then, slowly, the feeling of her presence in the statue dissipated and he knew she was gone. His tears fell upon the face of the stone goddess.

PYGMALION HAD PREPARED a surprise for his goddess. He had spent most of his meagre savings just days before to buy a yearling bull, as white as the ivory statue. Early in the morning he rose to collect his offering and gild its horns with gold paint. He placed flowers around its neck and led it to the birthplace of the goddess. He saw other devotees making pilgrimage along the road, but the two-day journey was not crowded. There was nothing on that western shore but the temple marking where the goddess rose from the sea.

On the morning of the festival, a tired old priest took the bull by the horns and led him to the altar. As the sacrificial blade fell against the throat of the beast, Pygmalion fell to his knees and praised his goddess, thanking her for all she had blessed him with. Then in supplication he prayed.

"Oh, Goddess Aphrodite, whom I love from the depths of my heart, hear this prayer from your servant. If I cannot be with you eternally, grant that one day I might find a wife who is the living likeness of my ivory girl. I have fallen in love with you, my goddess. Grant me, I pray, an outlet for that love."

The priest fell back as fire consumed the bull in three hungry gulps. Amazed he looked at the sacrifice as it was accepted by the goddess. "Your prayer is granted, faithful servant," he said in a voice that was not his own.

Pygmalion rose from the altar thanking the goddess and rushed back to Amathus.

PYGMALION ARRIVED AFTER a total of five days to and from the festival. When the first of the Propoetides fell in step beside him, he purposefully ignored her, but she said nothing. He was barely through the city gates when her sister joined them. And as he walked toward his studio, each of the daughters of Propoetus joined the procession. Pygmalion saw the youngest of the sisters waiting on the temple steps. She hesitated and then followed a few steps behind. Still the sisters said nothing so he continued to ignore them even though people had lined the streets as the procession progressed.

Pygmalion was too happy to be concerned. His goddess had granted his prayer. He did not know where, how, or when his wish would be granted, but he would have a wife approved of and given by the goddess. Nothing could diminish his joy.

The Propoetides followed him into his studio and silently ranged themselves around the room in front of the uncut blocks of marble. Pygmalion looked at them as they stood with a faraway look in their eyes. Almost by habit, he stopped in front of his ivory statue and bent to kiss her lips. He knew they would be cold, the goddess having left days ago. But to his shock, the lips softened and parted, accepting his questing tongue. He pulled back, suddenly conscious of the sisters encircling him. The eldest looked at him, her eyebrow raised in question. She turned and stepped into the stone. He watched her settle into her form, lift her eyes in wonder, and become the stone. The chips fell away and there was only the statue of the priestess.

He kissed the eyes of the ivory maiden and they fluttered open, looking at him with love and compassion. Nearby, the second sister dropped her robes and entered the stone, instantly locked into a pose of passion, embracing an unknown lover. Too excited to pay attention to the sisters, he stroked his statue's hair and felt the silky strands beneath his fingers. The third sister entered a stone. He touched the cheeks and a blush arose there as the fourth sister became a statue. His lover's throat swallowed as he caressed it with his lips and the fifth sister was absorbed into marble.

This progressed. He stroked the shoulders and arms of the statue and as they became flesh, the sixth sister became stone. He lovingly pressed the statue's breasts beneath his hands, suckling on their nipples, and the seventh and eighth sisters entered their final resting place. The ninth and tenth sisters became stone as Pygmalion massaged the supple flesh of his statue's legs. With a catch in his breath, Pygmalion stroked the statue's sex and heard her gasp as her moisture dampened his fingers. The eleventh sister entered the stone and froze.

Pygmalion looked at the eleven statues and his eyes fell upon the twelfth sister, Sephane. She clutched a drawing to her breast as she looked at him and then at the marble before her. Pygmalion reached out his hand to his bride and she grasped it. Sephane flinched, let the drawing he had done of her flutter to the floor and stepped into the stone. Of all the statues of the Propoetides, only one had a blemish — a tear-streak down her cheek.

Pygmalion turned to the ivory white maiden holding his hand. He bowed and kissed her fingers, now warm flesh and not stone.

"I am Galatea," she said.

"I am Pygmalion," he answered.

"Oh, I know you. I have known you since the first day you caressed the ivory stone. I have kissed your lips as you lay with me. I have welcomed your love from the moment of my awakening."

"But the goddess…"

"Was there with me, but I was there with her as well. I have looked into your soul, Pygmalion. I have listened to your dreams. I have felt your love. And now you have given me my freedom."

Pygmalion was thrown by this statement. Given her freedom? Of course, she was locked in stone and he freed her from it. It would be wrong to claim her as his own. He slowly released her fingers and bowed deeply to her — not as he would prostrate to his goddess, but as he would respect a perfect woman.

"I hope that you will think kindly of me now that you are free and not be repulsed by my treatment of you when you were stone. If I may be of service to you, please call on me at any time."

"Any time?" Pygmalion nodded. "Now?"

"Why of course. I'm so sorry. Here you are just awakened and have nothing! I've caused you to stand exposed to my eyes. Please forgive me. Whatever you need, if it is mine to give, it is yours." He snatched up the blanket wrapped it around her shoulders, regretfully covering her perfect features.

"I suppose that if I'm to be a member of polite society, I will need clothes. But perhaps there is one thing that you will be unwilling to give me since I am nothing more than stone to you."

"You are so much more than stone to me, fair Galatea. I could deny you nothing."

"Then may I have your love, Pygmalion? I assure you that there is nothing of stone left in me. My heart beats with passion. Hot blood flows through my veins. And though my skin is ivory white, I feel a blush rising in my face when I think of what I want from you."

"Galatea, you are truly the answer to my prayers. I will love you and honor you all our lives. I did not dare hope that you would feel that way for me."

"My darling, I have lain on a bed of marble for weeks awaiting this moment. Please, show me what it is like to lie in your arms on your bed. I am free and I freely give myself to you. I am yours, my love."

"IS IT READY at last?" Agathos demanded of his *kyrios*.

"Pygmalion and his wife await you in the *peristyle*, My Lord."

"A wife yet. And this is the man who swore he would touch no woman of woman born. She must be something else."

"Your Grace, you might not want your wife to be there when you see her the first time."

"You are right. I want this to be a private showing. I have twelve naked women waiting in my garden. Stay here. I'll go on alone."

The prince entered the central garden around which the rest of his palace was built. Two beautiful stone women graced the entrance to the garden. He stopped to look at them closely. That one looked familiar. He ran his hand up her leg and across her ass. Yes. Very familiar. He looked at the other and could not keep his hand from rising to her breast. Cold stone, but still silky and sensuous. Pygmalion had outdone himself. He worked his way into the garden crossing from one side to the other to touch and closely examine each stone woman. Exquisite. Simply exquisite. At last he made it to the farthest corner of the garden. There Pygmalion waited with the most delicious woman the prince had ever seen. Next to them was the most beautiful of the statues, yet she looked almost sad.

"Your Grace, please be careful with this one. She is fragile," Pygmalion said.

"Yes, of course. They aren't... playthings." The prince tore his eyes from the beautiful woman next to the artist. He could almost sense relief in the garden. "You have done well, Pygmalion. I understand you have married."

"Thank you, My Lord. This is my wife, Galatea."

"Congratulations." The prince was tongue-tied as he took the offered hand of the woman. He was very glad his wife was not present. "Ah, well," he said, releasing her hand. It was obvious that it did not belong in his. "I am pleased to make your acquaintance. You are just what our fine artist needs for his next commission."

"My Lord, we have not yet settled this one. I have delivered to you what you requested, have I not?"

"Yes, of course. I believe your next 'commission' will be the payment you seek. I understand you were recently at the birthplace temple."

"Yes, My Lord," Pygmalion said, remembering the message of the goddess and the acceptance of his sacrifice.

"The priest there has suddenly retired. He claims to have seen the goddess and instead of sitting in the temple he has gone into the countryside to evangelize the people. That leaves the temple untended. Really, we can't have that. It is much too far away for me to reach with a protecting hand."

"I had no idea," Pygmalion said. He was appalled. A temple with no priest?

"The stone merchant, Thanos, has informed me that you are on very good terms with Aphrodite. He mentioned this upon presentation of an exorbitant bill for the stone he provided. Don't worry, I'm pleased. These stones are magnificent. Almost real. Nonetheless, Thanos has said he is moving to Paphos and taking delivery there of his next shipment of stone. He has quite a following of people who have agreed to accompany him. In fact, it appears to be the founding of a small city-state. I have called you a prince among sculptors, and I promised you a kingdom of your own. That kingdom is the new city-state of Paphos. There you will become the new priest of Goddess Aphrodite and oversee the renovation of her temple. To amply reward you for your service, I will provide a small contingent and supplies for your fledgling theocracy for five years. By that time, you should have your city well under construction and the incoming citizens converted by your itinerant evangelist should make it a profitable adventure. In five years, I will journey to your new home and make sacrifice to our goddess. At that time, we will greet each other as equals."

AND THUS IT happened that Pygmalion and Galatea moved to the western edge of Cyprus to tend the holy shrine and establish the city-state as Aphrodite's first priest-king. Ten months after her awakening, Galatea bore Pygmalion a son whom they named for his home, Paphos. It was he, a devoted priest-king after his father, who walled the city of Paphos. A year after his birth he was joined by a sister, Metharme, known as the most beautiful young woman on the island next to the ivory lady, her mother.

Pygmalion and Galatea lived to a ripe old age and Pygmalion carved a giant statue of Aphrodite that looked out over the sea and her birthplace. In their old age, Pygmalion still looked like a young man and Galatea looked as pure and perfect as the day she was created. They held each other in their arms, even on the day they died.

Pygmalion Revisited

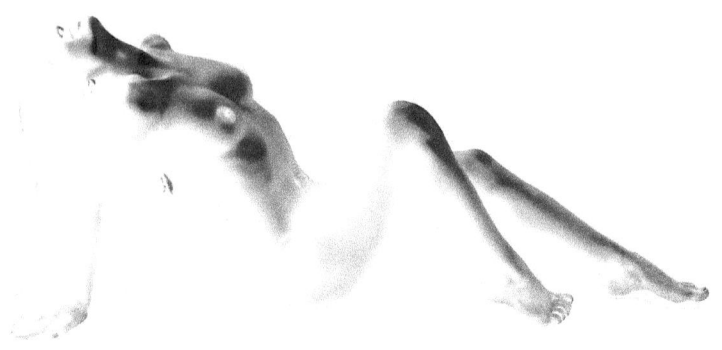

In the last book of the Model Student Series, **The Prodigal**, I introduced an artist by name only who had cast a metal crucifix for the Jesuit chapel Tony and Kate were working on. Tony created frescoes and Kate mosaics. But the crucifix was deemed an equally incredible work of art.

Though we never meet Jerome in person, we are left with the impression that he is an unusual and somewhat reclusive student artist at the Pacific College of the Arts and Design. This is the story of Jerome Z.

LOST WAX

I'M JEROME. No last name. I don't use it. *I* can't even pronounce it; I can't expect anyone else to. I'm an ethnic 'Heinz 57 Varieties.' Why the patrilineal line had to come from the only place in the world where you could have no vowels in a word is sheer bad luck. Imagine a name like Zgrdznk. No, that's not my name. But if you saw it and asked how it was pronounced, I'd just say "Smith. The 'Z' is silent." I got sick of it. When I turned eighteen, I found a judge who could sympathize but he insisted that I at least use the last initial. "Jerome Z," he said. "But you can still tell everyone that the Z is silent," he repeated my joke and smiled. I accepted that.

I started here at PCAD—that's the Pacific College of the Arts and Design—three years ago. Of course, now we're a part of Seattle Cascades University and I've just had my cast aluminum crucifix installed in the new Church of St. Jerome. I really don't care what school my degree comes from as long as I have opportunities like that. I came here for one reason only. I promised my mother that I'd get three new letters after my name. Next year I'll be Jerome Z, BFA. I chose PCAD because they only have twelve credit hours of general education credits required. Everything else is in my field.

Oh yes, my field is 3-D Visual Art. My medium is anything I can afford, but I pretty much prefer bronze or other cast metals. Anything durable enough to last a few centuries also happens to be weighed by the ton. I like marble, but talk about hard to move! I don't care for wood-carving. I don't feel like fired clay is permanent. I sculpt for eternity. I don't want to think of someone dropping a plaster bust and saying, "Oops." My sculpture will crack the floor if you drop it. If you can pick it up.

My story really starts a couple of years ago. I'd come to PCAD because they offered me a special grant to pay for materials. Marble block costs anywhere from $500 to $2,000 a cubic meter. Bronze only costs $10-$20 per pound, but you have to pay a foundry to cast it after you provide the wax mold. At PCAD, we can cast small items, hardly more than jewelry. There's an industrial foundry in SODO that will cast for a pretty reasonable rate. If you really want art quality casting, though, you have to go up to Bellingham where there's an art foundry. I guess the sum total is that whatever the medium, it's time-consuming and costly. And durable. That's why I'm a sculptor.

"WHAT GOOD WOULD a bunch of letters after my name be? Do you intend to get a PhD in sculpture?" Ms. Brock asked me pointedly. *Bitch.*

"I don't need letters. I'm an artist."

"Oh? And why do you think I need those letters?"

"You're a teacher."

"Ah. I see. Artists don't teach."

"Why would they?"

"Some of the most famous artists in the world also taught. In many instances, they referred to it as taking an apprentice. Sadly, they don't offer letters for apprentices, so you wouldn't get your BFA. And your master wouldn't release you for at least ten years. You plan to be out of here in four."

"That's what college is for."

"Exactly. College is for getting letters after your name. It has nothing to do with whether you are an artist. You'll come out of here knowing less than any apprentice who managed to get journeyman status and thinking you know it all."

"I promised my mother I'd get the degree. I don't need it to be an artist."

"And you expect to learn your craft—no, I'm not talking about the art—to learn the craft, the tools, the materials, and the techniques from books? From someone with letters after their name? In my class, you are the apprentice. Even if *eventually* you prove to have more artistic talent than me, you will learn the craft from me. Until you show yourself to be enough superior to me to teach this class, you will continue to be my apprentice—even after you graduate. Letters after your name be damned. This is the assignment for this class."

"But I want to cast something larger. I have a wax model almost finished."

"Do it on your own time and pay for it yourself. You have not shown me that you deserve to be trusted with more than half a pound of bronze. Our maximum capacity in the studio is one pound. For more you would have to take your work to Bellingham. The piece you propose is too big. Fulfill the assignment or fail the course." Ms. Brock pointed empirically at the door and I left.

Well, that went well. How was I going to cast anything out of bronze that weighed half a pound? This was stupid. Last term they gave me a six-inch block of marble to carve. How can you do anything remotely human in 216 cubic inches? Now if they'd given me a slab fifteen inches square and an inch deep, I could have done a relief. Most people did an abstract to show that they could polish a stone in a fairly consistent shape. I chipped away more stone than the others and by positioning the block on an axis that was diagonal through two corners, I managed a respectable if somewhat stylized human figure. Marble wasn't made to do miniatures—at least not with a chisel. I could have used a Dremel with a grinding wheel and put the detail in that I wanted. I'll probably do that later, just to finish the damned piece.

One-and-two-thirds cubic inches of alloy to melt and cast. If I hammered that, I could make a relief that was a good six inches square — maybe more. But it has to be cast and I knew that part of the test would be on being sure our mold wasn't too big for the amount of metal being cast. Damn, this was a bitch.

"YEAH?" IT WAS the best I could do to answer the pounding on the door. I wasn't interested in getting up. I'd managed to have a private room in the dorm by getting a doctor's referral that my sleep apnea would be aggravated by having a room-mate and that said roommate would undoubtedly also suffer. It was fifty bucks a month extra, which was a laugh because the room was too small to be used as a double, even if you went back to the old-style bunk beds. Whoever it was didn't get the message and pounded on the door again.

I dragged myself out of bed and threw the door open snarl-ing, "What?"

"Jerome, we're getting a group together to go to the sculp-ture gardens and thought you might like to go," said a small mop-topped brunette. "Oh, my God! You're naked."

"Yeah. So what. You got me out of bed."

"Wait! I want to see!" yelled a voice a few feet behind the brunette. Joyce. I finally managed to get a name to her.

"Whatever," I said standing there. "Girls are such sluts."

"I'm not a slut!" Joyce declared.

"I am," the blonde behind her said. Gloria. They were room-mates two doors down from me.

"Well, if you're satisfied, I'm going to get dressed and go to the studio. I've been to the sculpture garden. Several times. I need to work on my wax casting."

"Don't you want payback? You showed us yours. I'll show you mine," Gloria said, elbowing Joyce aside.

"Whatever," I said. She peeled off her shirt and stood there topless. I kept staring her in the eye, even though I was taking in her big tits.

"What?"

"I'm naked."

"Shit." She hesitated for a minute then started to unfasten her pants.

"Hey! We having a naked party in the hall?" A guy yelled from down the hall.

"Double-shit," Gloria swore. She grabbed her shirt in front of her and rushed back to her own room. I closed my door and went to the bathroom. With the water running, I thought about what I'd seen. I really don't want anything to do with girls, but I like to look. they are the substance of classic sculpture. I'm not gay, I'm just disgusted with the sluts. I wondered if Gloria had a boyfriend who would consider her exhibition cheating. Out of sight, out of mind. That's what my one-time girlfriend would have said.

When I was dry after my shower, I popped open the big jar of modeling clay I kept on my desk. It took a few minutes to get it warmed enough to work, but it wasn't long before I was sinking my fingers into the soft, cool mass.

This was what got me started on sculpture. Play-Doh in kindergarten. It was the feel of the clay that made me start sculpting. I let my fingers explore the curves my eyes had seen when Gloria stripped off her shirt. She was saggy. Her boobs weren't so big that she should have them hanging so flat. I bet she used to be a chub. She lost a lot of weight and the skin was sagging. There wasn't enough fat there to support it anymore.

Let's see. A good surgeon could probably lift them and tighten them. Of course, if she gained a lot of weight again, the scars would stretch. Too bad. My fingers kept molding and reshaping the clay boobs in my hands. Her nipples weren't bad. If the boob was just shaped a little more like this... I looked at what I'd been working on. Man! I'd used the same amount of clay but just reshaped it a little. That was a nice-looking tit. It just wasn't hers. I put it carefully into my sealed bowl to look at later. I might want to cast it.

I SPENT SATURDAY working with clay in the studio on campus while my classmates scattered to wherever college kids go on the weekend. One and two-thirds cubic inches of bronze. The spruing would take up about half a cubic inch of the bronze we were allotted. What remained would be the shape we cast. The expectation, of course, was that we would cast a simple shape, showing our understanding of the concepts and mastery of the skills for creating a mold and preparing it for pouring. We weren't expected to create any great art.

That's what pissed me off. It seemed like such a waste of time to create a mold and pour a bronze that wasn't worth anything but being melted down for the next class. I don't create things to be melted down and recycled. I create art. It's meant to last a thousand years. This seemed so senseless.

I went back to my dorm with nothing to show for my day's work in the studio. It was Saturday night and the dorm was dead. I flopped back on my bed and stared at the ceiling. As so often happened when I was alone, I started thinking of Beverly—the girl I left behind. Maybe I should say the girl who left me behind.

Damn it! We had so much going for us. I thought we had everything going for us. I was ready to can the whole idea of going to college and just get married. I even had a job offer at the foundry. We could have made it. Then she went and fucked it all up.

"Jerome, I'm in love with Phillip. I'm in love with you, too. But I want both of you."

"You want what?"

"I want you and Phillip to share me. I'll give you my virginity because we've been together so long, but I don't want to lose Phillip. You can deal with that, can't you?"

No. Hell no! Deal with the love of my life wanting me to share her with a guy I didn't even like? *The fucking slut.*

Needless to say, I didn't get her virginity. I didn't get anything. *Women. Fucking sluts.*

I tore the plastic wrap off a fresh block of clay and started kneading it, punching it like it was bread dough. Making it softer and softer. I loved the feel of the clay in my hands and could feel her taking shape. As soon as I saw Beverly's face in front of me, I punched it flat and started working the clay again. If I was going to make a woman, she'd be perfect. Everything about her would be perfect. She'd have a beautiful face, beautiful hair, beautiful breasts, beautiful ass. She'd be perfect and loyal and loving and true and smart and faithful.

The knocking on my door started. *Shit, I hate living in a dormitory.*

I opened the door and Gloria was standing there.

"You're dressed," she said, smiling.

"Uh... I wasn't in bed yet."

"I came by to... uh... can we talk? I brought a bottle of wine."

"Sure. Come on in. How was the sculpture garden yesterday?"

"Okay. I'd love to have your opinion on a couple of the pieces, though. I'm not a critic. I just want to make something beautiful. I'd like to know what I'm missing in a couple of them. I think ceramic is going to be my medium. I don't have aspirations to have things in gardens and parks. I just want to make cool things, you know? I'm babbling, aren't I?"

"Yeah." *Stupid girl.* "Um... why are you here? I mean, don't you usually go out on the weekends?"

"I called in sick."

"Called in to who?"

"My job. I don't go out on the weekends. I go to work. It's embarrassing."

"Hey, it's okay to work. I'm a little envious. I had a trust set up when my dad died and got a grant to pay for materials. But when it comes down to it I don't really have any money. What do you do?"

"Can we talk about something else?"

What the fuck? I thought I was being polite. "Sure. What's on your mind?"

"Something happened... between us."

"Yeah. You flashed your boobs at me. I remember."

"You were standing there naked when I did."

"Joyce got me out of bed."

"I got you up."

"I guess." Even though that wasn't true. I never get up. It was a good pun, though.

She poured us each a glass of wine after she looked all over my room for glasses. I got them out of the bathroom. I don't *need* two glasses in the bathroom, but there isn't any place else to put them, so I keep them both there. I'm not even sure why I have two glasses except that Mom equipped my dorm room. That's why there's a popcorn popper under my bed still in the box.

"Cheers. Look, Jerome, this is weird. All day yesterday and today something weird has been happening. I mean really, really weird."

"What?"

"My breasts got all tingly."

"Um... I don't know what to say about that."

"This is so weird. Did you do something to me?"

"Aside from looking at them when you flashed me. I don't remember making them tingle and I'm pretty sure I'd remember that."

"I just... I can't explain. It's..."

"Yeah, I know. Weird. Okay. I worked voodoo on you. How's that sound? I made a clay model and stuck pins in your breasts. Does that make it less weird?"

"No. You're really a bastard, you know?"

"Yeah. I figure that's the way I am." It was strained. I figured she'd just get up and walk out, but instead she changed the subject.

"Did you figure out what you are going to do for the bronze casting class?"

"No. One-half pound of bronze. Can you believe that? It's a thimbleful."

"Could you show me how you do your wax model?" she asked. Well, there's nothing I like more than talking about what I do when I'm sculpting.

"Actually, I don't start with wax. I use clay." I grabbed the lump of modeling clay I'd been softening and started kneading it as I spoke. "I do the model in clay and build the mold from that. I had a cool project outlined for a bust, but Brock said it was too big and I had to use the prescribed amount of bronze and work from there. It's so bogus."

"You're so sure of yourself. I'd be scared to death to start with more than the half-pound. I probably will never do anything bigger than this. But I'm really trying to get a technique down that will work. I thought we had to do the model in wax. I didn't realize we could use clay."

"Well, wax is okay if you like it, but it only gets so pliable and it only gets so firm. With clay, you can work it until it's as soft as you want and even add a little water to it if you need it looser. If you let it dry out, it gets hard. You can even fire it if you want a permanent model. Until you let it dry, it's pliable."

"What if you make a mistake?"

"You can keep reshaping it until you get it right. Like yesterday. After you guys woke me up and I took a shower, I sat down and started just working the clay. First thing you know,

I've got a breast that looks like yours and then I started reshaping it and making it perfect."

"My breasts weren't good enough for you."

"They're good enough for you. They just wouldn't work on a sculpture. They didn't have the right shape." I looked up, realizing that I'd probably just insulted her. But hell. She had to know her tits were floppy. What I saw surprised me. Gloria was taking off her t-shirt. There was nothing on under it.

"Are these the breasts you modeled in clay?" she asked. I hoped she didn't think I was going to fuck her, just because she brought wine and took off her shirt. I didn't even like her that much.

"Yeah," I said automatically. Then I glanced at her tits. Something was wrong. Or right. I'm sure I remembered her tits being a little saggy. The tits I saw on her chest were firm and round. Almost perfect.

"My breasts tingled all day yesterday and today," she said. "Not just my nipples where all the nerve endings are, but the whole breast. And then my underwear started getting uncomfortable. It didn't fit right. I put on my favorite bra this morning and it didn't fit. What did you do to me?"

TRUTH WAS, I didn't have the foggiest notion. I modeled that tit after what I saw on Gloria's chest and then just made some adjustments so it would be perfect. What I was looking at now was pretty much the perfect tit I sculpted.

And for the first time in over a year, I started to get a hard-on. Not since Beverly decided I wasn't man enough for her. I was still pissed about it—angry and bitter. I wasn't willing to let any woman get close to me. Every time I looked at a woman I got mad instead of aroused. I thought of going to a counselor, but I didn't want to talk to a man about sex and was repulsed by women. Rock and a hard place. It didn't make a difference.

Sure, I guess I missed masturbating a little, but I just wasn't going to be "that" guy.

Still, looking at Gloria's tits, they were pretty much perfect. She didn't need to strap them up in a bra anymore, that was for sure.

"I don't know what to say, except that they're perfect," I said after a while. "You're welcome, I guess."

"What do you mean, I'm welcome? You changed my body! Without my permission. Who do you think you are? Who are you to decide what is perfect and what isn't? Everybody's going to know. They'll think I had surgery."

"How is everybody going to know? Do you go around showing your boobs to everybody?"

"Yes."

"Huh?"

"It's my job, you fuck. I'm a stripper."

"Yuck! Do you know how disgusting that is? You just take your clothes off for money? Women! Shit."

"Yeah. But I notice you've been sitting there with a boner ever since I took my shirt off and never once suggested I put it back on. Little double standard, isn't it? I suppose you're a boy and that's the way you are supposed to act. Get a hard-on for everything with legs and boobs. Just like any other male."

"I don't either. I never do. I guess until now."

"So, you want me to put my shirt on so you can preach to me some more?" I just shook my head. I never wanted to see her cover those. They were just so... perfect. "What do you mean you never do?"

"I never get a hard-on. Until now."

"Never? Come on. Are you gay? No. Androgynous? Asexual?"

"I... I don't think I want to talk about this."

"No way. You're sitting there looking at my tits with a hard-on. What did you do?" I really didn't believe this. I popped the lid of my sealed plastic container open and lifted the modeled breast in my hands.

"You've molded that lump of clay to look like my tits. You *are* working Voodoo. I can feel you touching me. What are you doing?" She ran down. I sat there looking at the clay breast I was holding in my hand. It really couldn't be. I had to find out. I pinched the nipple lightly then smoothed it back into shape. Gloria gasped.

"Right or left?" I asked.

"Right." We stared at each other. Then she jumped up and grabbed the clay out of my hand. She looked at it and down at herself then smashed the clay back into a shapeless lump. "You don't touch any part of my body without my permission. Do you understand? That includes in clay." I nodded. "Say it! Say you won't touch me, even in clay, without my permission."

"I won't touch you and I won't model you in clay without your permission."

"Thank you."

"You're welcome."

"No. I mean thank you for these. They were a shock, but I love them." I smiled a little. "Before you make any more adjustments to me, though, I'd like to get to know you better." She shoved the clay into its can and sealed it then took me to the bathroom and started scrubbing my hands. That's one thing about working with clay; your hands get covered with a fine film of it. It takes a bit of scrubbing to get it off, but I'd never had anyone else wash my hands for me. And she'd never put her shirt back on. Nor had my erection gone down.

When I was clean and dry, she led me back and pushed me down to sit on the bed. She kept hold of my hands and brought them to her chest—to her soft, warm, perfect breasts. It was magical. More magical than thinking that I might have changed her by modeling her in clay. She still didn't let go of my hands. She guided them in exploring the complete surface and moved my thumbs across her firm nipples. I could feel her shaking — or I was shaking. I couldn't tell which. She scrunched up her eyes and gasped and I felt a warm flood in my pants.

Shit! I just came in my pants! And by the looks of it, so did Gloria. She let go of my hands but didn't take them off her breasts. "Better than clay?" she asked. I looked down at the spreading wet spot in my jeans and nodded. As I looked up I saw that she had a wet spot on her crotch as well. Gloria pulled her cell phone from a back pocket and dialed. "It's Haven. Let me talk to Rick." There was a pause as she waited for someone. I was getting uncomfortable sitting in my sticky pants, but I'd pretty much have to push her out of the way to move. And I smelled something, too. I'd never smelled a woman's arousal before. Her wet crotch was only a few inches from my nose and I found myself leaning forward, letting my hands slide from her breasts and wrap around her waist. "Rick? It's Haven. I just want you to know that I quit. I can't come back.— No. Things have changed. Just give the clothes in my locker to the other girls. I'm not coming back. I can't do it anymore." She closed her phone and stuck it back in her pocket then backed up. I lost the intensity of her aroma and the feel of her skin.

"Why did you do that?" I asked. "I mean quit your job?"

"Jerome, I like my breasts. I didn't used to care. I thought my boobs were ugly. I thought men were stupid when they tried to drool on them. They flopped around and guys loved to fold a dollar and put it under them. But that all changed today. I don't want anyone near them now." She hesitated. "Anyone else. I'll go now. I think I should go change my teabag. You too." She leaned in to give me a little kiss on the cheek, grabbed her shirt, and rushed out of my room.

I STILL COULDN'T believe I'd really had anything to do with the change in Gloria's breasts, but my damned erection wasn't letting me forget her. The old porn question, "Does your wang ever go down?" Answer: "Not if you don't fuck with it."

You might think I'm abnormal, but I'd never actually touched a girl's bare breasts before. I'd fooled around with Beverly a bit, but she'd kept me outside her clothes. The day after I refused to share her, she was no longer a virgin and Phillip had his hands all over her. I looked at my hands. I'd held the world's most perfect breasts in my hands. I could still feel the nubs of her nipples pressed against my thumbs. They were tight and full, but not the rock hard tips that you hear about. Supple, I guess you'd call them. They were like the tip of a cock and not like the shaft. Man. Even more perfect than I imagined.

I ripped my mind away from Gloria and tried to focus on my stupid final project again. I'd heard that the school's hot-shot star faced the same situation last year. He had an idea for his final drawing project and then found out he had to jump through a bunch of hoops to meet the standard his art teacher set. Something about having to use a specific model. I had to admit, that mural in the admin building hallway was hot. They made a big point about how a freshman had done the art when my class went through orientation. Now the guy—Tony Ames, I think they said his name was—was over at SCU painting some big-ass mural on the side of their gym. I can just imagine living in his shadow for the next two years before anyone notices what I'm doing.

Anyway, legend has it—Christ. How can you become a legend in one year?—that he did the project the art teacher required and that's what was selected for the mural. But he also did the piece he wanted to do for the Gala. It made a big splash. So, I guess I could waste my time doing what Brock wants me to do for my casting and then do a real one to exhibit in the Gala. That would be kind of cool. Problem is that you can get canvas and paint for like a hundred bucks. It would cost a min-imum of $500 to get my casting through the foundry. And I'd have to go to Bellingham to get it done. I could do it, though. I could even do multiples and have a limited edition. Maybe five. That would bring the cost each down to about $200 and I could sell them for $500 each.

I'm not all that mercenary and I know that the chance that I'd sell five sculptures for $500 in the next five years is pretty remote. But I know the school isn't going to release grant funds for my personal projects for another year at best. I don't have a lot of money to fund my own stuff.

So, it looks like a miniature for my class project. I cut a cube of clay out of my block a little more than an inch on a side and started molding and flattening it just to see how thin I could make it and what kind of shape I could mold out of such a little scrap. It was pitiful. Two inches square by a little more than a quarter-inch thick. A kindergarten snake about a quarter-inch in diameter and ten inches long. This was going to be tough. I squeezed the clay into a ball and started softening and shaping it.

When the doll's face appeared, it was good but it revealed a flaw in my plan. Working the clay this thin, made it floppy and hard to hold the shape I would need to create the face out of a solid lump of clay. That would make getting the thickness of the wax pour perfect. This project was going to be a lot of work, but at least the little doll face that I'd created would make the project better than a throw-away. I looked closely at the face, making sure it didn't resemble Gloria. Too much. I'd promised that and even though I was anxious to do some more experimenting, I had to respect the fact that I would be experimenting on a human—even if she was a woman.

FRIDAY NIGHT ROLLED around and I was in my usual position—sprawled on my bed staring at the ceiling. Ms. Brock had approved my project and I was ready to dip wax. I'd do that on

Saturday since I didn't have any other plans. While I got tense when I was focused on my projects or a particular sculpture I was working on, I really didn't have any stress in my life. No girlfriend. No social life. No drugs. I just lie in my bed looking at the ceiling and listening to music until something moves me to start modeling clay. Still, lately I kept seeing the same thing and I didn't dare reach for the clay. I'd promised.

There was a light knock on my door. I opened it to find Gloria with two glasses and a bottle of wine.

"Want to join me?" she asked before pushing her way past me into my room. Wait. I'm supposed to join *her* but she's coming into *my* room? Women! Oh well. I found I didn't mind her company.

"Uh, sure. Come on in," I said as she plopped down on my bed. She handed me the bottle and corkscrew.

"Mind doing the honors?" I put the bottle on my desk and started working on it. I thought they made wine with screw tops these days. It took me a couple minutes to rip up the cork enough to finally get it out of the bottle. I turned back to her to get the glasses. She was sitting cross-legged on my bed with no shirt on. Damn! Her tits are absolutely perfect. I wasn't sure I remembered them right by Wednesday, though I'd been thinking about them regularly all week. It looked like my memory was accurate. They were damned perfect.

"You, uh… miss your job?" I asked.

"Huh?"

"You're topless."

"Oh. Yeah. No, I don't miss my job. It's kind of a relief. It's not like a girl really wants to spend her weekends getting pawed." Shit. How many guys had had their hands all over her breasts in that club. "You know, it's different now. It just seemed natural to take my shirt off when I'm with you. Do you mind?"

"Gloria, I'm looking at the two most beautiful breasts that God ever created. I don't mind."

"Let me tell you, Jerome, the two that God created were nothing to write home about. The two you gave me, though... It's like I should show them to you because they're yours in a way." I poured the wine and we sipped a little. I was going to sit in my desk chair—intended to—but somehow ended up sitting cross-legged in front of her on the bed. I could almost reach out and touch... "Did you see how I dressed all week?" she asked.

"I saw you in class. You had jeans and a sweatshirt on, I think."

"Think nothing. You know it for a fact. I dressed that way all week. I felt like I was hiding a little bit. I haven't felt like that since my boobs started growing when I was thirteen. It was like I didn't want anyone else to see them. Only this time, instead of being embarrassed by the knockers that were hanging from my chest, I wanted to keep these a secret that only the two of us knew. I mean, I even managed to shower and dress in my room when Joyce was doing something else so she wouldn't see them. But I walk in here and the first thing I wanted to do was take my shirt off."

"Thank you. It... uh, well... don't be offended, but I can't help but respond to them—to you."

"I'm not offended. I'm really proud." Awkward silence, but neither of us moved to hide anything. "Jerome."

"Gloria," we spoke at the same time and laughed. I nodded to her.

"Can I model for you some more?"

"Are you sure?" It was what I was just going to ask her.

"I think so. I mean, I know I'm not perfect. Even Joyce has a cuter face than me and that woman that models for the fig-ure-drawing class, Lissa, is a goddess. But I just think you see me differently than... I am."

"I've been thinking of you all week," I confessed. "When you knocked on my door I was lying here in bed staring at the ceiling and imagining your face."

"My face? Tired of my boobs already?" she laughed. It didn't sound like a happy laugh.

"Gloria, are you uncertain about your breasts or what they do to me? God! What have people done to you?"

"People," she huffed. "You mean men? Listen, you are the first guy I've felt like spending time with since forever. I finally decided if all I was ever going to be was something to be passed around from boy to boy I was going to get paid for it. That's why I started stripping. I needed the money. Men are pigs. Most men I've known would get hard when they saw grapefruits in the grocery store. I hated my life, my body, and everything. In the club, I'd just build a false persona and go with that until my shift was over. I'd pick myself up at the door when I left. You could have been a customer of mine and I wouldn't have recognized you in class. I don't have a very good self-image. And I know you are really critical."

"I'm some bastard, aren't I?" I said. "Here I think of every woman as a slut because of what my girlfriend did to me and you think of all men as pigs because of what they did to you. I'm sorry." I meant it. Maybe I'd been carrying around this woman-hating long enough. It certainly wasn't making me happy. In fact, sitting here with a half-naked Gloria was the closest I'd been to happy in a long time.

"Quite a pair. Jerome, it wasn't you. You didn't do all those things to me. You gave me these. It's the first thing about my body I've been happy with in years." She reached for my hands and I put my wine glass on the floor by the bed. She pulled my hands to her beautiful perfect breasts. "And I'm not her. When I said these were yours, I meant it."

When you are sitting cross-legged facing a woman and both your hands are held out in front of you on her chest, it's awkward to lean in for a kiss. We managed it, though it was bizarre. After the first attempt, I scooted around so my back was against the wall and Gloria moved up next to me so we could kiss and fondle at the same time. We made out for about fifteen minutes. This was the first make-out session I'd had in over a year and the best one ever in my life.

"What do you like?" I asked as I drew slow figure eights around her breasts. "I don't have any idea what I'm doing."

"Well, I know I don't like to have them pinched. I almost slugged you when you pinched the nipple on the clay model last week. Other than that, though, all I know is that I like you to see them and touch them."

"I'm afraid I'll get too excited and go off in my pants again. You've got to help me slow down, Gloria."

"Do you still want me to model for you?"

"Yes. I have this idea for a face..."

"Before you go playing with my face, would you do my hands? Jerome, I trust you, but I'm more than a little scared. What if I came into class Monday looking like someone else? When you make changes, you'll go slowly, won't you? Please?"

"Whatever you want, I'll go at whatever speed you say. Somehow or another you've become... important to me. I can't get you off my mind. Now, why do you want to model your hands?" She held her hands up together fingers spread and palms out so I could look at them. Her left hand was ordinary. Maybe her fingers were a little short in proportion to her palm, but not bad. The right hand reflected the left except for the thumb. It was different. Odd.

"No doctor could ever say why, but my right thumb is more like a big toe. It's a good thing that people don't pay attention. I mean, even you who can see me and mold me in clay, didn't notice that I have a big toe for a thumb. I guess that's the effect of having bare tits in your face, though. You can't see anything else."

"And you want me..."

"To fix it. That way I'll know for sure. I'll know you molded my body and gave me these breasts. There really isn't any other explanation. When you eliminate the impossible, what remains—no matter how improbable—must be true. And I... I so want to be perfect for you."

"I honestly didn't do any voodoo or anything. I don't know how it happened, but I'm more inclined to think there was some freaky coincidence and act of nature at work. At the same time, I love touching you. I'll do it."

"How do you want me to pose? Just with my hands on the table or something?"

"No. How about you lie here on your left side. Here. Use my pillows to prop yourself up so you don't hurt your neck."

"Why do you have so many pillows?"

"Oh. I guess I've always been like that. I like to lie on my side against something, so I use this big pillow against the wall so I can lean back into it. Then it takes two pillows to prop my head up so it isn't dangling on my shoulder. I stick the small pillow between my knobby knees so I don't bruise them against each other. The other two are mostly so I can sit in bed and read and stuff." I arranged pillows around her and got her propped up. As I arranged her, I took every opportunity to touch her and caress her breasts. She seemed to really like it. I finally got her posed and put her right hand on her stomach, just below her breasts. Then I got my lump of clay and started working it while we talked.

It was great to have Gloria lying on my bed topless 'modeling' for me when I was only working on a clay model of her right hand. I connected with her hand, but I kept looking at her face while we talked and laughed. Well, her face and her tits. But mostly her face. I saw something behind what people would normally see when they looked at her. It was something in her eyes. Yes, her nose was a little crooked. Her lips were a little thin. Her ears stuck out just a hair too far. But in her eyes, there was a kind of fire that made you forget about all the little imperfections as if they weren't there.

She was giving as good as she was receiving, too.

"So, your girlfriend wanted to be the meat in a sandwich and you turned her down? You do know that's the stuff porn movies and male fantasies are made of, don't you? You should at least have taken her cherry."

"When I found out she wanted someone else—anyone else—it just all shut down for me. I couldn't have gotten hard for her if she was... I can't even think of a situation that would normally turn me on. There just haven't been any."

"But I turn you on, don't I? I mean, there was evidence last weekend that we affected each other."

"Gloria, I won't deny that. But seriously—you won't believe this of an 18-year-old male—that was the first time I had an orgasm since Beverly made her suggestion. Hell, I think it was the first time I had a hard-on."

"You've still got one, you know."

"Yeah. Well, I'm still staring at the world's most perfect boobs. I don't understand what's gotten into me." I stopped and looked at what I'd been working on. The clay in my hands was smooth. I'd worked it with my fingers as much as possible and then used a stylus to put in details while we were talking. Geez! I'd never really done model making while I was talking to someone. The detail in what I'd made was incredible. It was like holding a living hand. The fingers were long and elegant, but not freaky like some alien. The length of the longest finger was exactly the length of the palm. Everything was proportional. While I looked at it, I imagined what it would be like to hold that hand if it were flesh and blood. I could almost feel the blood pulsing in it; feel the sweat as my palm contacted hers. I liked this. I liked it a lot. I trimmed the fingernails just slightly. I think girls put those long fake nails on because they don't think their fingers are long and elegant enough. This hand didn't need extra-long nails. It was perfect.

"Jerome?" I realized I'd been silent a long time, caught up in my little fantasy. "Let me see, please."

I showed her the beautiful hand I'd made. There was no big toe for a thumb. The fingers weren't short and stubby. The palm wasn't thick.

"It's beautiful," she whispered. She took a deep breath and held her hand out beside the clay I held in mine. She still had a big toe. Still had stubby fingers. Still had a thick palm. I could hear a catch in her breath as she turned away from me. She pulled on her shirt and stepped toward the door. Before she reached it, she turned around and kissed me softly. I could see a sparkle of tears in her eyes. "I guess you can go ahead and do my face if you still want to," she said. She was gone before I'd finished saying goodnight.

ALL NIGHT I had dreams. Maybe I should say I had nightmares. There were sure enough dismembered body parts in them. A breast floating here, a hand there. Lips. Eyes. Ribs. The curve of a hip. Mixed in all that were sensations that I'd felt either for the first time or at least for the first time they meant anything. A kiss. How does a kiss feel? What perfect lips and teeth and tongue could make me feel like I had just run a marathon or something? How could a simple glob of fat held in my hand become a perfect breast that made me hard? How could those supple nipples call so fervently to my lips?

I woke up in a sweat with fresh cum on my stomach. A fucking wet dream? I looked at my clock. Four a.m. on Sunday. I took a shower and then went back to bed. I got up again. Nothing would be open for breakfast. Starbucks didn't even open until eight on Sunday. But I was awake. I sat at my desk and grabbed a fresh lump of clay out of the bucket. In front of me on the desk was the hand that I'd made last night. I still looked at it, but I was thinking about kissing Gloria. My hands were busy, molding those lips. It was the softness that made lips perfect. The softness let them mold to my lips. Tongues were clumsy by nature. Lips were flexible and sensuous. Tongues were slippery and wet. Lips were moist and full, and welcoming. If not for the lips, the tongue would have no place to go.

I finally fell back asleep, leaving the clay untended on my desk.

I SAW GLORIA in class Monday afternoon and she looked happy. That was a relief. We didn't sit near each other, but I really liked her and I was glad she wasn't bummed out. I knew the whole thing about me manipulating or changing her body was impossible. I'd proved that spectacularly on Saturday night. I found myself with a sudden longing, though, that it would be Saturday again and she'd come to my room with a bottle of wine. I should ask her. If she didn't come over, I'd be miserable. Maybe I should ask her out. But what if she doesn't really like me and was just coming to get body work done? I wanted desperately to kiss those lips again and to touch those incredible breasts.

I screwed up the spruing on my wax mold and had to break it off and start over. I finally finished and got the base coat of sand and plaster sprayed on it. When class ended, I was ready to quit for the day. To my delight, Gloria walked up as I was putting my project away.

"Is that my face?" she asked.

"This? No! It's a doll. I promised I wouldn't work on your face without your permission and this project has been going for two weeks. Even if I took your statement Saturday night as permission, I wouldn't have been able to get this far by now." I turned to look at her and pick up my bag. There was something in her eyes. Excitement? Laughter? Happiness? Maybe a little of each. While I was looking at her I quickly screwed up my courage. "Would you like to go out with me this weekend? Maybe to a movie? Or dinner? Anything?" She smiled at me.

"That would be great, Jerome." We turned to head out of the classroom and she slipped her hand into mine. It was so natural. So perfect. Her fingers intertwined with mine and I brought them to my lips to kiss. She held them in front of my face when I'd finished kissing them and I looked at them. Beautiful, elegant fingers on a perfect hand. A perfect thumb. It was my left hand, so the hand I was holding had to be her right. I turned it over in both my hands and stroked her palm right up her wrist. Her hands were beautiful. I faced her and she kissed me. "I love you, Jerome," she whispered.

SOMETHING ELSE WAS different about Gloria. She never mentioned the change in her appearance again. If I brought it up, she brushed it off with a comment like, "I was a late bloomer." On the other hand, we were spending a lot more time together and I was really liking it. I had a study partner, a lunch partner, a dinner partner. We even worked in the studio at the same time and I gave her some hints on getting a good even shell on her mold. In the evenings, we'd go to my room and as soon as we got there her shirt would come off. Mine, too. We did get some studying done amidst a good make-out session every night. Not every session ended with an orgasm, but a few did and they were spectacular.

Friday night we went to Dixie's Barbecue. It was a warm evening and the sun had shone during the day. In Seattle, they say the five stages of Winter are denial, anger, bargaining, depression, and April. Gloria wore jeans and a sleeveless t-shirt with a light jacket. Apparently, I got the memo and was dressed pretty much the same. I didn't look nearly as good, though.

We laughed and talked all through dinner.

"So, what are you going to do with your degree?" I asked. "Are you planning to become a sculptor?"

"No way. I think it's important to get a well-rounded look at art in all dimensions, but I'm not like you. I like to work with clay most when it's spinning on a wheel."

"Pottery?"

"Yes. I know it's a craft and not an art, but I really like enameled ceramics."

"That's not true. Ceramics are just as much an art as anything else. Sure, there is a long tradition of craftsmanship, but there is in sculpture, too. It's what you bring to the medium that makes it an art form."

"Okay but I'm still not going to hold up a clay pot next to a marble bust and say they are equivalent."

"I used to think that way," I said. "Something's different now. I used to think everything had to be perfect and cast to last a million years. But maybe some things aren't meant to last that long."

"You mean like our class projects for casting?"

"Well, I guess. Ms. Brock made a good argument. And I'm beginning to understand some of what she says. It's just contrary to my nature to try to make something that I don't think is perfect."

"Are you excited to pour the bronze on Monday?"

"Yeah. But, there's something else. I've been working on that I want to cast, only I'll have to go to Bellingham and pay mucho bucks to get it done. I'm going to be borrowing everything I can from my grant to hire the foundry."

"What is it?"

"You."

"Go away."

"I'm serious. I've got the mold ready for two parts and want the third part complete if you'll agree."

"What's the third part?"

"Your face."

"I already told you you could do my face if you wanted to."

"I didn't want you to think I was changing you without your permission."

"I don't know what you think you can do to me, but knock yourself out."

That was weird. We already had the evidence of her breasts. They were perfect. If she wanted to, her hands were so beautiful she could do hand-modeling. She hadn't seemed to notice yet, but her lips were lush and full and not hard and narrow like they used to be. If I straightened her nose and tucked her ears a little, she would definitely look different.

The thing was, I didn't think she needed the nose and ear work. She was beautiful. But for my bronze concept of perfection, I wanted to make the changes. Ever since the night I modeled her hands in clay and she didn't see immediate results, it was like she didn't acknowledge anything happening at all. Well, we'd just have to wait and see what happened next. I paid for our dinner and we walked back to the dorm. The path led by Baby Dolls, the strip club she used to work at. She pressed against my left side so I was between her and the club.

"Hey, Babe! We've got a job for you. Bring your boyfriend in and we'll get him a dance while you go strip on stage."

"Get lost, buddy," I snarled at the guy.

"Wait a minute. That's Haven. You don't know what you've got there kid. If she hasn't given you a lap-dance and rubbed those big sloppy titties in your face, you haven't lived."

"Go away, Rick. I quit. I'm not coming back."

"Hell, come on. You know you want to get out of those clothes." He stepped in front of me and into Gloria's personal space. I didn't think. I reacted. I shoved him back.

"Leave her alone," I commanded. He didn't answer. He slugged me in the gut.

I'm no athlete. Sure, I'm in pretty good shape, but just being in shape doesn't mean anything when you get a fist full force in the gut. I doubled over. I heard a scream.

I should rephrase. It was like a siren going off in my ear.

"Police! Fire! Fire! Help!"

"Oh shit," the guy who slugged me said under his breath.

I was gasping for breath—couldn't get enough into my lungs—passed out. Flashing red and blue lights. Gentle fingers stroking my forehead.

"Fine. I'm fine," I mumbled.

"I think you are, but you threw up and aspirated some of it," a voice on one side of me said.

"Second time barbecue. Gah!" I said. "What a waste of a good meal." Laughter. Arms holding me tightly.

"We're taking you to the hospital. Better safe than sorry. He really sucker-punched you." The voice.

"I'm going with him." An angel. I realized the hand that was stroking my face was Gloria's beautiful hand. It was her voice laying claim to me. I really needed to tell her it was okay, but they were moving me and I was lifted into the ambulance. I still hurt, so I wasn't going to complain about getting checked out. Gloria was beside me as soon as the door closed. I've never been hit so hard in my life. Well, hell, I've never been hit. I'm an artist, for God's sake! I opened my eyes.

The inside of the ambulance was dimly lit. We were bouncing along. The EMT had a blood pressure cuff on me. I suppose she had to do something. Gloria was looking at me and crying.

"It's my fault. It's all my fault," she sobbed. "It's all because I worked in that hateful place."

"Shh. Shh. Sweetheart, it's all right. It's not your fault. You quit that life. You are free of it now."

"Did he hurt you, miss?" the EMT asked.

"No. Yes. He grabbed my arm after he hit Jerome. I was screaming and someone dragged him off me."

"Which arm? Let me see." Gloria pulled her jacket off her right arm and the EMT examined it. Even I could see it was turning black and blue.

"This is 454 calling home. We're bringing the young lady in with the man who was attacked. Her arm is severely bruised. X-rays and full test kit."

"Roger that, 454. We're standing by."

"I'm so sorry, Jerome," Gloria continued. "We never should have taken that street back to campus."

"Hey, no matter what the business or whether you worked there at one time, no one has the right to jump someone on the sidewalk when they're walking by," I said. "It's not your fault." She leaned down and kissed me. I kept my lips together. "Gloria, maybe you should wait until I get my mouth rinsed out before you do that. I don't even want my own tongue in there." We laughed and I groaned. He really did a number on my gut.

OF COURSE, AT the hospital, we were preempted by two guys with knife wounds. Since they were bleeding and we were just bruised, they got treated first. They made Gloria stay in the emergency room while they wheeled me down to get my ribs x-rayed. Yep. Cracked one, the bastard. When I got back to the little cubical, Gloria was looking frightened and I held out my hand to her but they escorted her out to x-ray. I laid there waiting like an idiot for half an hour. At least I could breathe now, even though it hurt to breathe deeply. Gloria walked back in with a doctor, a nurse, and a policeman. Sounds like the start of a bad joke, and for a minute it seemed like it might be.

"You, young man, have a cracked rib. You are going to be bruised, but there isn't anything we can do but give you a mild pain-reliever and tell you not to stress it for a couple of weeks. It will be sore for a while, but the scan shows no internal injuries that we need to be concerned with. The rib did just what it was supposed to do and protected your internal organs. Miss, your injury is largely cosmetic. A bruise and some abrasion caused by your jacket twisting on your arm. We'll write up the paper work and you're free to leave."

"What was your relationship with the man who allegedly attacked you," the policeman asked next.

"Allegedly?" I snarled.

"Just answer the question."

"I've never seen him before."

"Not you, her." I glanced at Gloria.

"He's my former employer."

"That's all? He claims you were lovers. In fact, that 'she'd fuck anything with a dick,' and that he'd fired you for hustling customers." This cop was an asshole.

"Just a minute, officer," the doctor broke in. "As is standard procedure, we did a complete rape kit on this young woman. What we found was unusual."

"You're going to tell me she was raped on the sidewalk?" the cop sneered.

"No. I'm going to tell you she's a virgin." That shut us all up. The cop stuttered for a moment then turned to leave.

"I have all your contact information from admissions. We'll let you know if anything comes of this," he said and walked out, followed by the doctor who was berating him for his lack of professionalism and insensitivity with a promise to report him to his superiors.

"Come on, you two," the nurse whispered. "Let's get you out of here and get you a taxi back to your dormitory. I have a two-day supply of your painkiller for you. Tomorrow is Saturday, so you might have trouble getting the prescription filled. I shouldn't have to tell you this since you are under age, but do not drink alcohol while taking this medication. Now, let's get you signed out."

WE WALKED TO my room and Gloria stood outside as I entered. I turned to wait for her.

"Do you want me to come in?" she asked. "Even knowing what a bad person I am?"

"From what I heard tonight, you are a better person than about anyone else on campus," I laughed. "Gloria, please come in. Please stay with me tonight. I promise I won't do anything, but I really want to be with you." She smiled at me. Wow! That smile is magnificent.

"Let me grab my toothbrush," she said. She went to her room and returned a minute later with her toothbrush and a towel. "I might want to shower in the morning," she explained. She sure wouldn't want to use my towel. I forgot to toss it in my laundry when I did it Tuesday.

We brushed our teeth and sat together on the bed. I leaned over and kissed her softly.

"Minty fresh," I said.

"Waste of good barbecue," she laughed, quoting what I'd said on the sidewalk. She kissed me again. "Can we cuddle in bed and just sleep together?" she asked.

"I'd like that," I answered. She hesitated for a moment and for the first time ever, I reached over and pulled her little sleeveless t-shirt out of her pants and over her head. She returned the favor and we pressed our naked chests together as we kissed again. I grunted a little as she squeezed me and she let up quickly.

"I'm sorry."

"It's okay. It was worth it." We kicked off our shoes and I unbuttoned my 501s. "Uh, I'll leave my shorts on."

"Okay. I'll leave my panties on." Let me tell you that my boxer briefs covered a *lot* more than her panties. It wasn't a thong, but they were cut high on the hip and the view was breath-taking. We cuddled into the single bed and kissed for a long time before we both nodded off to sleep, breathing each other's air.

THE DISTRICT ATTORNEY had been trying to shut down Baby Dolls for a long time. The club was grandfathered into a zoning ordinance that would have banned adult entertainment and liquor sales within five hundred feet of the college campus. It happened that on the opposite corner of the block the club was on, there was a building the college leased for storage of maintenance equipment. Technically, the Club was in violation. It was a political football. But the arrest of the manager gave the DA some leverage and he got a temporary injunction to close the club until the case had been heard. That assured him that the case would get to court instead of being held in an unending cycle of continuances and motions. We were deposed later that week. It turned out that just the visible bruising on Gloria's arm was grounds for a second count of aggravated assault against the owner, instead of just one for me. Of course, the DA didn't care about us. It was just more leverage against the club.

In the meantime, I was working on the clay model of Gloria's face. I knew better than to do everything all at once, so each day I spent some time focused on just one little aspect of her features. We poured our bronzes and I started work on my new creations. They were a little strange. I had one breast and part of a torso, one hand, and the face I was working on. I thought I'd overdone it when Gloria met me in class with her hand covering her nose.

"Are you okay?"

"My nose itches. I think I must be allergic to something."

"Let me see." She moved her hand away from a perfectly straight nose, just the right size for her face. I kissed it.

"You look like a Greek goddess."

"Don't be silly. No. Please go ahead and be silly. I love to hear you talk about me. I think you are a little crazy, but I love it anyway.

MY BRONZE BABY-FACE came out pretty good. I filed off the spruing and the rough edge where the halves of the mold came together. I was happy that I managed to save the mold. If I was doing something like this, I wanted to make it count. I had three more molds that I was taking up to the foundry in Bellingham and figured I might as well take this one, too. What was another $500 or so? I just hoped the molds were good enough to yield five castings each.

Gloria had a final project to finish, so I made my way up to Bellingham on the train by myself. I was on board by 7:30 and caught a cab to the foundry at 10:00. I was a scheduled pouring, so after the guy examined my molds he set them up. The bronze was already melting.

It was a smaller place than I expected. The crucibles were large enough to pour a good-sized statue, I figured, so Gil, the owner, said he'd pour all four molds and after an hour we'd be able to open the first one. He had two assistants working with him and had me in an apron and gloves as well. I figured this was great experience for me as I put the four molds in the kiln to heat them before the pour. The molds would come out at about 1100 degrees Fahrenheit, which would still be about 600 degrees cooler than the molten bronze when it came out of the furnace. As I was pulling the ceramic molds out of the kiln, Gil was skimming the sludge off the top of the bronze. His two burly assistants were wrapped in more layers of apron and gloves than I could believe. They even had welding helmets on. Gil guided them and they lifted the crucible on its pulley and poured.

I could hear the sizzle as the bronze filled my molds and smell the heat as the bronze met the ceramic.

There was a lot of work to be done while the first casts cooled. The temperatures of the furnace and the kiln were checked, the crucible refilled with bronze shavings and the melting process repeated.

The cast of the baby-face came off fine but the casting wasn't very good. There were a couple holes and it was rough. The bust was no problem. The four pieces of the hand were touchier, but Gil managed to pry them off without damaging the mold. Sadly, the mold for Gloria's face broke and was not reusable. I was distraught, but it wasn't anything Gil could have done better.

"Well, that wasn't bad. We could get one more casting out of each of the molds except the face, of course. Or we can step back and do it correctly."

"What?"

"It's rare that we can get more than two casts out of a ceramic mold. It's too hard on them and they stick to the bronze, even though you did a good job with glazing and hardening them. But they are rigid. You can't get them off the bronze without damaging them. Look at the face you created. Which is nice, by the way. But look at the folds for the hair. The area we have to work the mold free of is smaller than the part that has to be pulled away. So, what we usually do for limited editions is make a vulcanized rubber mold. Because it's contained in a rigid frame, it can't bow out with the weight of the bronze, but at the same time when it's cool, it's flexible enough that we can pull it out of the tight places."

"What do we need to do?"

"We take your original bronze and pour the rubber over it to make a mold, much like you did with the original wax model. The difference is that you have an original bronze to start with instead of number one of a set. Your documentation should show that this is cast from a ceramic mold and the mold was broken. Then you do the numbered edition in the rubber molds. We can change the thickness, too, so things like the little face aren't so fragile."

"How long will this take?"

"We can get the rubber molds done this weekend and then pour at our leisure."

63

I agreed to the process and watched my bill for the art go up. Well, I could live on less this summer. If it was really good, maybe I could get approval to advance more from my materials grant.

MS. BROCK LOOKED over my bronze originals and examined them carefully.

"And you are doing an edition?" she asked.

"I had the molds made, but I ran out of money before we could pour any. These were all cast from the original ceramics."

She reached out and tentatively touched the hand. I saw her shiver.

"Jerome, I don't like saying this to any student." I froze. She was going to criticize this? Who the fuck did she think she was. The bitch was just a teacher. I started to tense up and was ready to explode when she continued. "You have to know these are extraordinary works. Beautiful. Just beautiful." Huh? I thought… "So, what I'm going to ask will probably sound stupid, but that's my job. Can you go without selling them for a while? And without casting the limited edition?"

"Uh… why?" Clever.

"There is a feeling that this work, taken as a whole, is not yet completed. Have you considered additional pieces in the suite?"

"Well, sure. I wasn't going to do a full-body casting because it's too big to sell. I was going to do a foot. A hip. Maybe…"

"Yes. Just what I meant. Here's the thing. There are two parts to making a masterpiece. We used to say one, do the painting and two, hang the artist. But the fact illustrated is that there is the art and the business. The artist doesn't have to be dead to make the art valuable, but complete art is much more valuable than partial. If you can wait to sell pieces until the suite is complete, the perceived value to your buyers will go up."

"I guess I see the sense in that, but I kind of used all my living money for the summer to cast the originals. I was hoping to make that much back."

"Your grant allows some amount of discretion to be exercised. Usually, a project would be brought before your committee prior to investing cash in the casting. But, I believe I can drive approval to get you reimbursed for this and to pay for the casting of the rest of the originals. When it comes to casting the limited edition, we might have to find some means of paying without the grant, but with the originals complete, that might be done with a subscription. The problem is, you wouldn't get a subscription for a partial."

"You think I could get reimbursed my expenses, though?"

"I believe I can probably even cover creating the molds as part of your class practicum."

"I guess that would be great."

"Now, how did you intend to display these for the gala?"

"Display?"

"Yes. They look great, but they won't really sing if they are just lying on a table. How do you see them when you imagine them on display?"

MS. BROCK WASN'T kidding about the work not being complete after the bronze was cast. Let's face it; I'd never considered them as separate pieces. They were all part of one beautiful woman. But putting one hand, one breast, a face, and a doll in positions where the viewer would see them as a single composition was a lot trickier. Of course, whenever I looked at them, I saw Gloria. I knew exactly how far each piece should be from the next and at exactly at what angle.

When she understood what I intended, she wasn't that bad to work with. I packed each piece with clay and once I had them in the correct positions, I inserted a one-inch Plexiglas rod into the clay to make hole for later. Then we fired them all in the kiln. The kiln is only 1100 degrees and the bronze doesn't lose integrity until you top 1800 degrees, so there was no danger in heating the castings. I secured the rods to a plywood base and once the castings were cool enough, I was able to push them onto the rods. When you stepped back, you could see the entire figure, almost as though certain parts were invisible.

I managed to finish just a few hours before the preview of the gala.

WHEN I REACHED my room, the door was unlocked and I looked in cautiously. Gloria sat on my bed in nothing but a pair of bikini panties. God! She looked good enough to eat and the more I thought about it, the more I liked the idea. Of course, we hadn't really gone past kissing and almost naked making out. We'd both had orgasms, but we never touched each other's privates with our hands.

I entered quietly and she jumped up off my bed and into my arms. I caressed her back as her breasts pressed into my chest and we kissed.

"Do you have a tux for tonight?" she asked.

"Um… no. I couldn't afford to rent one after I paid for the castings. Ms. Brock said I should have a reimbursement by Monday, so I won't have to keep eating instant Ramen noodles," I laughed.

"Did you check your closet?"

"Why would I…?" It slowly dawned on me what she was saying. I opened the closet and sure enough, there was a tux hanging in a plastic bag.

"I hope it's all okay. I took your suit with me and they matched the sizes."

"You didn't need to do that," I said.

"Yes, I did. I have a perfect dress and needed my date to look just as perfect." There was something haunting about those words.

THE GALA WAS cool. Of course, the focus of the whole thing was some big-assed mural that Tony Ames was painting on the side of a building at SCU. Gloria and I stood and stared at it for a minute when we finally got to the front of the crowd. People were tossing donations in a box for the homeless. The mural was good.

"What are you thinking?" Gloria asked me.

"I like it," I said. "But it's so... two-dimensional. And big. I'm sure at this scale we're not getting the impact of how huge the people are on the side of the building. Not that I'm knocking big. A lot of sculpture is super-sized. It's just... flat."

"Well, that was concise," she laughed. "See them over there? That's Tony Ames and I hear that both the women with him are his girlfriends. Well, two of the women. Geez, there's like eight of them standing around him."

"Yeah, well women are..." What was I going to say? Sluts? Hadn't I learned anything from being with Gloria? ". . . unpredictable." I finished lamely.

"I don't know. I predict there is going to be one sleeping with you tonight."

I froze. Did she really mean...?

"Just sleep, but I don't want to be apart from you tonight, if you're okay with that. I'm not... We're not ready for that next step yet." She turned and stroked my face and I lost myself in her eyes. "But soon," she whispered.

We wandered into the freshman exhibit and I was pleased to see several people standing around my sculpture. An older couple was looking at it closely. I stood behind them and listened.

"Look at the lips, Bob. I'm not into women, but even *I* want to kiss them."

"Clarice, this artist has passion I haven't seen in bronze in a long time. You need to sign him. He's definitely in the review. What did you say his name was?"

"He just goes by the name Jerome. I don't know if that's an assumed name or if that is all his legal name actually is."

"It's actually Jerome Z," I said from behind them. "But the Z is silent."

"And are you Jerome?" the guy asked.

"Yeah. This is my girlfriend and model, Gloria Edmonds."

They both stared at Gloria for longer than I thought an introduction should take. After he'd scanned her from head to toe, the guy turned and did the same scan of my bronze. He didn't stop at the torso that was sculpted. I saw him close his eyes and follow the shape the rest of the way down, nodding. Finally, he turned back to me.

"I'm Bob Bowers, syndicated art critic. This is Clarice Bortelli, an artist's agent. She represents two of your fellow students."

"And if this is an example of what you can do, I'd like to discuss representing you as well," Ms. Bortelli said. "This is a gala and I've no intention of harrassing you with questions and a sales pitch. Here's my card and if you think you might be able to produce more work like this in the future, please give me a call. I'd like to see more."

"Thank you, ma'am. Sir." They turned and moved away.

WE SLEPT TOGETHER. We kept our shorts on—well, my briefs and her panties, but the rest of our naked bodies were pressed together. We didn't grind ourselves into each other or try to come. We just held on to each other. Sometime during the night,0 I woke up and found my cheek was wet where it was touching hers. I looked at her, thinking she was crying. Then I realized the tears were coming from my own eyes. I wiped them on a corner of my sheet, but I lay there awake, staring at the ceiling for a long time before I fell back to sleep.

What if I wasn't perfect for her?

THE GALA IS the last event of the school year except graduation, and I had no reason to attend that. I was satisfied to know I was no longer a freshman.

Gloria and I spent the day talking about the future.

That was scary. We'd avoided that topic ever since the first time she'd pulled her shirt off in front of me in the hall. We'd just lived in the moment. The more Gloria talked about her hopes and dreams, the more I realized that not only was I not perfect, I wasn't even appropriate. When she asked me about my future I just laughed and said I wanted to be Michelangelo. She didn't laugh.

"Who hurt you so much, Jerome? Do I ever stand a chance of winning you?"

"Um… winning me?"

"I keep thinking that I'll prove myself to you and you'll really love me, but you pull away at the last minute. What else do I need to do? I… I love you."

The tears I'd shed while we slept the night before came rushing back. I couldn't help it. I sobbed. She held me against her naked bosom while I cried. When I could speak, I couldn't look up at her. I guess I said just about everything to the nipple that was right in front of my face.

"I hated women because of what she did. I decided that if she was a woman that all women must be like her and I wouldn't have anything to do with them. Then I got here to PCAD and my advisor is a woman who doesn't even have an advanced degree. But she's forced me to comply with the system and has taught me more about being an artist than any art teacher I've ever had. Then you came along. It was all an accident. I didn't mean to come to the door naked. I had no idea you'd just take off your shirt in front of me. And I certainly had no intention of sculpting your breasts. Then you posed. I did your hands and your face. Everything about you came out perfect." I was barely coherent. Tears were still pouring out of my eyes and I didn't care. This is where I was going to lose her. This was where she would realize what a total asshole I was and dump me flat.

"Everything about you is perfect and I'm not. Just a guy who models with clay and wax. You put me in a tux last night so I would be worthy of you. Well, I'm not. I want to model the rest of you. I want to explore your body and cast it in bronze, but I know that when I do it will be too good—too perfect for the likes of me."

She held me, rocking for a while and shifted just enough that her left nipple was against my lips. The little baby I felt like started sucking. She sighed. I fell asleep with my lips on her tit and tears still in my eyes.

"GO GET A shower, sweetheart," she said when I woke up. "I'm going next door to shower and I'll be back in a little while. Jerome. Wait for me. Don't leave." I sat up and she grabbed a t-shirt to pull over her head before she went out into the hall. I stumbled into the shower and just stood under the water forever. I finally managed to shampoo and wash, then grab my towel. I could hear the shower next door still running.

I flopped in my desk chair with the towel on my lap and stared at my bowl of clay. I heard the door open and Gloria came back in. She stripped the shirt off and there was nothing else on her body. Her pubes were smoothly shaved. Her legs glistened and I thought she must have used some oil on her body. She turned and arranged the pillows on my bed while I watched her butt. I realized I only had a towel draping me.

"Get your clay out, Jerome," she said as she lay in the position that I'd used for the previous pieces. "I want you to keep modeling me. Only please don't make me perfect. Just make me perfect for you. Please." I could see her eyes misting. I smiled. Perfect for me.

I stood up and let the towel fall. It wasn't the first time Gloria had seen me in my altogether. She glanced, but brought her eyes back up to mine. I sat on the edge of the bed and reached my hand out to touch her. I closed my eyes and let my hand trail down her side and over her hip. I slipped along her leg all the way to her foot. I heard her sigh and felt her shudder as I drew my hand back up the inside of her lower leg and slowly across her sex. I'd never felt a girl's sex before — not skin to skin. I thought about it. I thought about how it would feel if it were not my fingers exploring. I still had my eyes closed when I stood and took a step toward my desk. I knew my cock was standing out rigid, but I didn't care. She turned me on and I wasn't going to hide the fact from her.

I grabbed my lump of clay and started shaping it. When I opened my eyes, I looked straight into hers.

"This is going to take a while, and I'm going to need more clay." She smiled.

"I don't have any other plans. Do you think you could finish sometime in the next fifty or sixty years?" We laughed.

What I realized when I had touched her, let my fingers explore her legs, feet, and sex, even going back up to her left elbow tucked against her side and across her breasts, was that I knew what was perfect for me. I'd listened to her talk about her plans and desires. What was perfect for *me* was what was perfect for *her*.

IT *DID* TAKE a long time. Not fifty or sixty years, but all summer. My grant provided for housing and meals and studio use all summer, so after a brief trip home to see the folks, I was back in my room. Gloria continued to have the room next door over the summer, though she was never in it. The single bed was a little crowded, but I didn't mind having her sleep partly on top of me. I didn't mind at all. I'm not sure when it was that we just fell into bed without having bothered to put underwear on after a modeling session, but I woke up the next morning with a very hard cock sandwiched between her thighs.

We still didn't make love. I think we were both having too much fun just pretending to act naturally while we were walking around nude most of the time. I was walking around with an erection. And there was a certain smell in the air that I'd learned to recognize as Gloria's arousal.

There's something different about the way a flat artist sees a model and the way a dimensional artist sees her. I mean... This is hard to explain. A flat artist has a real connection with his model; there's no doubt about that. But the connection goes through a pencil or a paintbrush onto the medium. If you think of the difference, I was molding clay with my fingers. Yes, I had some ribs and scrappers, and even a fettling knife for some detail work. But most of what I do is with my fingers. So, think of having your fingers in warm moist clay while you shape it like a girl's breast, or hip, or... pussy. I'm sitting there looking at the model and my fingers are working to get the same shape and feel and my cock is getting hard.

That was the piece I was working on the first time. I had the clay in my hands molding—sculpting Gloria's pussy. I was hard as a rock and finally had to set the clay down and close my eyes for a minute. While I was sitting there in my chair, I felt Gloria's hand on my erection. I opened my eyes in time to see her tongue come out to lick me, then her mouth opened and I watched my cock disappear as I felt her tongue and lips sliding over its surface. She never looked at me during that first blow job. She was totally focused on my cock. She'd lick and then look at it. Suck and then check to see if it had changed. She stroked my length and then stuck out her tongue to trace the same path her hand had taken. Besides being so turned on I knew I would come in seconds, I was fascinated just to watch her learning about my cock. It was almost like seeing it for the first time myself.

I warned her I was coming and she sat back with her hand on me and watched as the cum fountained out of me.

"Wow," she whispered. She went into the bathroom and brought back a washcloth to clean things up. "Thank you," she said when she was finished. "That was so... Thank you." *She thanked me?* We kissed and she settled on my lap for a long time before my sticky, clay-coated fingers started to irritate her. She led me to the shower and after we washed each other thoroughly, we went to bed.

The next day as we settled in for another session, I sat on the edge of the bed where she was posed and ran my hands around her body like I did every time. When I reached her sex I looked at her and raised an eyebrow. Her thighs relaxed and parted as my hand moved inside her hidden zone for the first time. I held her cradled in my right arm as we kissed and I stroked her sex with my left hand.

I'd been around the outside of her lower lips with my fingers, but I'd never delved between the folds. The instant moistness reminded me of the clay, but this was much warmer — much slipperier. And she was much more responsive. I didn't have time to go down on her that first time. Before I could get away from our kiss, her thighs clasped together, trapping my hand, and she screamed into my mouth. It wasn't like a life-threatening scream, but I bet that if anyone had been outside our door they'd have wondered if it was an emergency. Thank God, she didn't yell 'fire!'

The modeling of her pussy went better after that, but I didn't finish it until I'd tasted her and felt that glorious feeling of a girl coming on my tongue. And I had double work to do cleaning up. I'd come at the same time, all over the side of the bed.

I KNOW WHAT it sounds like, but we didn't spend the entire summer naked in my room. We'd have never survived if we had. Sometimes we'd take two or three days between posing sessions. Gloria had a job to go to and the terms of my grant indicated that I had to do work in the studio to get it ready for fall classes. I had to check supplies, clean crap off the floors, and do a lot of other menial jobs that were made much more pleasant by the fact that I'd sleep that night with a naked angel in my arms.

I also met with the Bortelli lady. What a pushy bitch. I caught myself responding heatedly to her when she was pushing for more pieces to see. I stood up from the table I was going to tell her to just shove it when she cut me off.

"Mr. Silent Z, you may be too much trouble for me to work with. I understand temperamental artists, but I have two who had spectacular debut showings in Seattle this spring and are working on their New York and San Francisco Christmas shows. I really don't have time to babysit. When you are ready to work, please let me know. If you'd like a referral to a 'man,' I know a couple who will swat your ass for you and make sure you toe the line. Your choice."

I was a little miffed and left in a huff, but the more I got to thinking about it, the more her requests seemed more reasonable. I called Tony Ames and asked him what he thought.

"Oh yeah. Hi, Jerome. Clarice told me you might call. How's it going?"

"Well, I'm not sure. I… uh… haven't signed a contract with her yet. I don't know if I can work with a woman."

"Why not?" He sounded like it was the most natural thing in the world.

"Well, I know you've got like a gazillion girlfriends and don't have any problem working with women, but I just respond to them in a negative way."

"You're gay?"

"No. It's not that. Believe me, I've got a girlfriend and we're making progress… slowly. But relating to women is hard for me."

"I don't know of any man who relates to women easily. For example, my wife Lissa…"

"You're married?"

"Well, not legally. We do have a legal partnership agreement, though. Anyway, Lissa about blew through the roof when her ex, Jack, suggested Clarice represent me. I didn't have a clue, but it turned out there was some bad blood from way back when Lissa was a young teen. The thing is that when Lissa settled down a little, she agreed that Clarice was the best choice for representation and they could play on the same team. To this day, I don't have a clue what happened and how they worked it out."

"But you work okay with Ms. Bortelli?"

"Oh yeah. She tells me what to do and I do it. Just like with any woman."

"Gee, thanks, Tony."

"Not a problem. Seriously. Think about what you want in life. What are your goals with your sculpture? Then take that to Clarice and ask her if she can help you reach those goals. Think about it carefully, because she will hold those up to you every time you fuck up and tell you if you aren't keeping up your end of the bargain. It's called accountability. To some degree or another we all have to accept it."

"How'd you get so smart about women, Tony?"

"Um… four girlfriends. Good luck, Jerome." *Four? Fuck!*

My next meeting with Clarice Bortelli was more successful and when she saw the clay models for the next phase of the suite, she agreed that I was on the right track and then proceeded to tell me that as soon as that batch was in production I should be thinking of what I would do next. She didn't want to go to a first showing with only one suite. I signed a contract and found that I was an artist with representation.

I took the clay models for seven more sections to the studio and began the process of making ceramic molds. The hardest part for both Gloria and me was working on the back views. I had her face, breast, and one hand. I added a foot, thigh, navel and sex. Then I sculpted her ass and one shoulder as seen from the back. She had to lie facing the wall with no support against her back while I did those. And while I was working on them, I decided I needed to do the back of her knee as well.

Have you ever really looked at the back of a woman's knee when it's slightly bent? It's like a thousand times more interesting than the front of her knee. When you are looking at the front of a woman's knee, you see it as just the pathway up to her pussy. But looking at the back, the two tendons that form that hollow behind the knee, the way it flows into the calf and up into the thigh—that was a real revelation to me. I *had* to sculpt it.

IT TOOK MOST of first semester in the fall to get the new pieces ready for casting. I had classes, too. Gloria came with me to visit my mother at Christmas. Gloria said her family was out of her life and we were not to consider a holiday visit. Mom liked Gloria and exclaimed about how beautiful she was at every opportunity.

"Jerome brings the best out in me," she told Mom. It was the only hint I'd had in months that she was aware of the changes that had occurred. When I had the opportunity to observe her interacting with other friends, like in the cafeteria, she seemed to stand taller, erect and confident. She was excelling in her pottery class and was preparing for an exhibition in the summer. She smiled at people and looked them directly in the eye. She was everything I admired in a woman. Perfect.

I had the shell ceramics done and was ready to wax them when Gloria and I passed the point of no return. She maintained the fiction of rooming with Joyce, next door to me. She never slept there, but used the room for her clothes and for times when she needed to study alone. Otherwise, we slept together every night. That night, we'd been petting a lot, including oral sex for both of us when we turned toward each other in the middle of the night and I felt her hand guide my cock to the opening of her sex. We'd both come a couple times already, but neither of us was ready to quit. I stopped as I felt the warmth of her fluids against the head of my cock.

"Are you sure, love?" I asked. "There isn't any going back."

"Do you love me, Jerome?"

"Gloria, I don't even have words to describe the way I love you. You are the most important thing in the world to me. You are the most beautiful and perfect woman I've ever known. Am I good enough for you?"

"You're a little on the dense side, but I think I can deal with that. Push into me, darling. I want you to be my first, last, and only."

That did it for me. It was like the magic words. Beverly wanted me to be her first, but then to have Phillip do her immediately after. Gloria only wanted me. I pushed and there was a little twinge as Gloria's maidenhead gave way. She caught her breath and held me in a death grip for a few seconds, then encouraged me to keep going. We had both come recently, so we weren't frantic to pump away. When I was deep inside her, we just held each other and reveled in the closeness.

It was so perfect.

I FINISHED THE casting of the originals and made rubber molds up in Bellingham with Gil. Ms. Brock came in to the studio to help with mounting the remaining pieces of the suite for our sophomore gala. When they were finished, the display was over five feet wide and two feet tall. It weighed about three hundred pounds. There were eleven pieces in the finished suite that made up the single original. I asked Gloria to come to the studio and see it before we took it to the gallery, so she and I were both there with Ms. Brock when Clarice and that Bob Bowers guy showed up. I was so proud to stand there with Gloria—my lover and my friend and my model. I know that there were some changes that had gradually occurred as I found out more about Gloria's body. She'd slimmed down a little in her waist and hips. I wasn't sure but what she'd grown maybe an inch taller since I met her but maybe she was just standing straighter. Everything fit together so well it was amazing.

They did a lot of nodding and wrote a lot of notes. They talked to Ms. Brock and pretty much ignored me. I was beginning to get a little pissed, but with Gloria there to calm me, I didn't say anything.

"This is good," Clarice said. "I think an edition of eight would be very good. We'll offer the original only as a complete set and reserve the first edition as a complete set. The other seven we can sell piecemeal."

I kept what Tony said in mind. "Let Clarice set the sales strategy and pricing. Your job is the artwork." Well, I hadn't made any money off this project yet, but my grant had at least paid for the casting of the originals.

"We'll do a presale with pictures from the original," Clarice continued. "That will give us commitments that we can borrow against to do the castings. But it would be good if you had a few other pieces ready to go at the same time. They don't have to be part of this suite, or any suite for that matter. We just need to show people that you aren't going away after this piece. The first one is going to increase in value over time."

"I especially like the baby," Mr. Bowers said.

I caught my breath. Baby? The little doll-face that I'd included cradled in her arm? I saw Gloria reflexively grasp her stomach. Mr. Bowers looked at us then looked down Gloria's body slowly like he had the first time they met. He looked back at the bronze. Gloria still had one hand over her stomach. Could...? Shit! All spring, neither one of us had thought once about birth control. I just assumed... Oh God!

Mr. Bowers had a soft smile on his face when he turned back to Gloria.

"Galatea," he whispered.

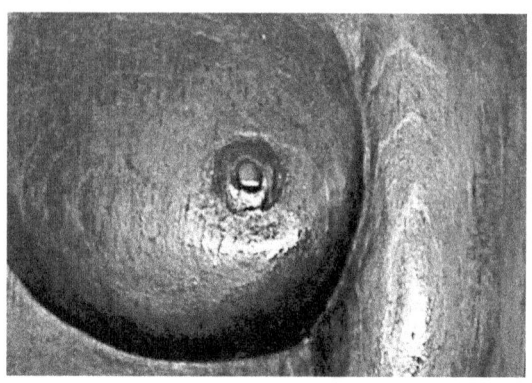

One needn't live for art to be an artist, nor does all art need to be a permanent fixture of public display. Like life, art can be transient, merely a bridge from one reality to another.

WHITTLED AWAY

*T*HE MAN *who chops his own wood warms himself twice.*
"You always have something clever to say when it's *me*
who's suffering." Nonetheless, David set another log on the chop-
ping block and swung his axe. It was a well-practiced swing of
the blade and split the log smoothly. He picked up the pieces and
tossed them in his wagon. He picked up the next log, almost too
small to split. He'd spent the past week cutting the wood to the
right lengths with his chainsaw. He'd hauled it out of the wood-
lot, but the larger pieces still needed to be split or they wouldn't
burn thoroughly. Some wouldn't even fit in the fireplace.

He stood with the stick of wood in his hand and let the
axe idle against his thigh. A limb had broken away from this
trunk many years ago, leaving a protruding knob, long-since
healed over with bark. The shape of the knot filled his hand
with memories.

I was never as firm as that. And never a wooden lover.

"No, my love, but the shape is about right. I held those precious breasts enough times to remember."

*I went to sleep at night with your hands supporting them. I felt
so secure.*

"I think I'll stop for now and go sit a spell."

*Don't forget to drink something. And I mean water, not any of
that cider that's gone hard.*

"I don't drink that stuff."

Don't lie to me. I know better.

"I suppose you are spying on me from the grave. I'll have
water first."

David dragged the two-wheel cart up to the house and stacked the load of firewood, keeping the breast-shaped log aside. He'd just keep that by his chair on the porch for a while. He pumped water and washed his head to cool off. The water was cold. October was already brisk and he was headed for a hard winter. As long as he kept a fire in the firebox, the pump shouldn't freeze. But he needed to finish splitting that fourth cord of wood and if he was smart he'd put in another. He drank his fill of the cold water and toweled himself off. There'd been no hard frost yet, so he figured he could do without a fire tonight.

Instead he fixed a simple dinner of rice and beans, cut a sausage into the mess, and sat on the porch with his plate.

Those cans of vegetables you put in won't do your body any good unless you eat them.

"Always complaining about the way I eat," he groused.

Just always want you to be healthy, my love. Was I really such a nag?

"I'd give my life to have you here nagging me now."

I don't think that was an answer. What are you going to do now?

"Hmm. Sit here." He rocked in his chair and picked up the log. Maybe he'd whittle a little. He pulled out his Buck knife and carefully began stripping the bark from the block of wood.

Ooh. Like the first time you undressed me.

"D, I'M READY, darling. I know I told you I wasn't ready, but I am. I was just scared."

"Ella, I would never hurt you. I'd never rush you. We don't have to do anything else right now if you don't want to."

"But I *do* want to, David. I want you to touch me and to… to see me. Kiss me and tell me how much you love me."

Nineteen years old and he was a bit scared, himself. David and Ella had grown up near each other and she went from being the bothersome neighbor kid to the love of his life in a matter of months. He'd tried going to college, but that didn't work out. He spent all his time writing home to her and none of it studying. When he predictably flunked out, he'd received his draft notice within two weeks. Tomorrow he would be headed for boot camp.

"I love you more than the stars in the sky, Ella. More than all the grains of sand on the shores." He kissed her and they lost themselves in each other's touch. "I love you higher than the moon and deeper than the ocean. I love you the very soul of my being." They kissed some more and his hand moved slowly to cup her breast.

"D, you make me feel like an angel lying in your arms — like I will be able to fly when I've given myself to you fully. Make me fly, love. Make me sprout my wings and soar into the sky with your love. I'm yours."

His fingers found the buttons on her blouse and slowly twisted them through the loops. She said she'd dressed for him tonight. That meant she'd worn nothing under the silky covering. She expected him to touch her unfettered breasts through the sensuous fabric. She hadn't expected him to peel it away from her skin when the night began, but there was nothing now that she wanted more.

David's tears were as hot against her skin as his tongue. He worshipped her as he slowly undressed her. She pulled at his shirt and his undershirt to get them off so they could like chest to chest in the bed of the old pickup. Every kiss reminded him that tomorrow he would leave — that tonight might be the only night they could ever share together.

She didn't complain when he found the fastening for her skirt. In fact, she helped, lifting her hips so he could pull the garment off her. She made sure her underwear went with it. From that point, there was not another doubt in her mind. She knew what she wanted as she unbuckled his belt and pushed at the waistband. He quickly got the message and in minutes they were lying against each other with no barriers. They kissed, stroked, and petted each other. She felt his erection hot against her skin and when it parted her wet folds and pushed into her sacred channel, she wept. This spot—this place she had kept so private—was meant only for her husband. David had never mentioned marriage, though his letters and his words had often enough spoken of love.

YOU SOILED YOURSELF, David.

"Not my fault, woman."

I didn't think men your age had spontaneous emissions.

"Shows how much you know."

Was it really because you were thinking about our first time together?

"The first and the second and the third. And how I miss you, Ella."

There, there, my handsome man. Let's clean up and go to bed. I want to hold you all night.

"In my dreams."

IF YOU ARE going to make my pregnant belly, you need a much bigger piece of wood!

"I didn't say it was your whole pregnant belly. I said it reminded me of when you were pregnant."

How? Tell me how.

"You never wrote to tell me you were pregnant."

What could you have done? You were in the army. They didn't give you leave to come home before they shipped you out.

"There was no time. We were at war."

But still you wrote.

"Every day."

MY DARLING ELLA,

They told me Southeast Asia was hot. They didn't tell me that the monsoons had come in and I was going to spend every night shivering in a hole, soaked to the bone. It's not that I'm cold. I'm scared, sweetheart. Charlie is all around us. Sometimes I think they shoot one shot, someplace way down the line, so we'll think there's a sniper crawling around picking us off one at a time. But in the morning, we're all still here.

Andy, my black friend, ducked down next to me last night and told me to paint my face black like his. Then to close my eyes and shut my mouth and Charlie wouldn't see me no-how. He's a funny guy. I hope we both make it back so I can introduce you.

Again, I'm thinking of that night before I left. You gave me a reason to come home, Ella. I'll get there. If I have to walk through hell, I'll come home to you.

Love, David

"DAVID, DAVID! DON'T die. Please don't die!" she screamed as she was finally admitted to the hospital room. "I love you! Please don't die!"

"I'm not dying, Ella. I just got more shrapnel in my leg than they allow. I'm home, darling. I'm coming home," he said as she hugged him. Every damned thing hurt. They'd shipped him to the VA hospital after he was patched up in Germany. They said he wouldn't lose his leg. That was supposed to make him happy. They said he'd never run a marathon but the only place he'd ever had to run was in the army so who the fuck cared about that. What they didn't say was that he'd be in pain every day for the rest of his life. Fuck them.

"I love you, David."

"I love you, Ella. You are what kept me alive over there. I had to come home to you." They hugged and he suppressed the wince. They said the piece in his shoulder was there to stay. They couldn't dig that out. But there was something different in this hug. "Ella? What's this?"

"That's our baby, David. Please don't hate me!"

"You never told me we were going to have a baby! When is it due?"

"Well, figure it out. We only had one night together. David, is it okay? I'm sorry. I... You don't have to marry me. I..."

"Don't *have* to marry you? What are you saying? Do you have someone else?"

"No! Oh no. I've never had anyone but you. I never want anyone but you," she wept.

"My sweet, sweet, love. You should have told me. I'd have got shot up sooner so we'd be married by now. Did you think that when I made love to you that it was just because I was leaving? I want you now and forever. I don't ever want to lose you, love." The two were wrapped in each other's arms, his pain forgotten for the moment. "Let me touch my son," he said. She crawled up onto the bed next to him so he could easily touch the roundness of her belly. He felt the bump of her navel beneath the maternity clothes she wore. "I thought you had an innie!"

"Your son pushed it out. He's already so big. Another month. Will you be with me, David?"

"You listen here, you silly girl! There's a chaplain here in the hospital. I want you to go find him and bring him right here to my room so we can get married. I don't want to wait another minute now that we're together. You go find him," he said.

"I can't, David."

"What? Why can't you?"

"You haven't let go of me."

PYGMALION REVISITED

SO, IT'S NOT my pregnant belly you've carved into that old block of wood. It's my popped-out belly button. Like one of those turkeys for Thanksgiving that has a button that pops out when it's cooked right.

"I thought for a while that it was permanent and you'd always have that outie belly button. How was I to know it would go back in after the baby was born?"

I'm sorry, David.

"Don't be sorry, darling. I miss him every day. Just like I miss you. Please tell me you're together now."

He's here, but he's got his own friends. You know how kids are.

"I should have been there."

You were a responsible father. You can't be everywhere at once.

THEY NAMED THE baby David Andrew. David for his father and Andrew for the army buddy who never made it out of the jungles of Viet Nam. Junior was born just a week after David got out of the hospital and the three of them lived with his parents. As a wedding gift, his parents gave them an acre that fronted on the road and was bounded on one side by the drainage ditch they called a creek. The little family spent hours that summer sitting under a walnut tree on the property and dreaming about where they'd build their home.

David went to technical school when he'd recovered enough to be active. He'd always been good with wood, so becoming a carpenter seemed like a natural choice. And he was good at it. Good enough that his instructors pushed him to keep going and become a cabinetmaker. He could get construction work during the summer and continue his schooling in the evening and during the winter. Education was something the government owed him. Each night Ella rubbed soothing analgesic into his shoulder. It was a surprise when they started getting disability payments from the government even though he was working part time. Payment for pain, his father said.

When Junior was three years old, they had a well dug. David and his father spent every evening digging out the trench that would become the foundation when they poured concrete and set the blocks for the crawlspace. The ground was too wet and unstable to dig a basement. David was a little relieved. The foundation was all they got done that summer, but until the snow flew, Ella and Junior walked hand-in-hand with him to picture themselves in their new little house. They stepped off each room, planted stakes in the ground to show where doors and windows would be, and sat on the ground together where one day they would sit on their front porch.

And at night, when the baby and the grandparents were asleep, they made love.

YOU ALWAYS COME back to that, don't you?

"Ella, making love with you was all I wanted to do in life. I didn't care about work or school. I cared about getting you in bed."

Or anyplace else you could get me. What's that you keep stroking there? It feels so smooth beneath your hands.

"Oh, nothing. Just whittling away. It kind of reminds me of a certain bit of your anatomy."

You are squeezing my little wooden ass, you old pervert!

"My, my, it does sort of remind me of that, now you mention it. So round and smooth. No baby's bottom had anything on you."

As you taught me out at the house site.

"We did have some good times out there."

And your parents knew. How many times could we ask them to watch Junior while we went out to the site to take some measurements? With a blanket?

"Seems you suggested it on a few of those occasions."

"DO YOU KNOW what Junior said today?" Ella asked as they walked hand-in-hand the quarter mile from his parents' house to where the cold foundation of their new home awaited.

"No. Do tell me what."

"He asked why he didn't have a little sister," she smiled.

"That child is three and a half years old, love of my life. I can't imagine that he even knows what a baby sister is."

"Well, he didn't say the actual words. I just knew that was what he meant," Ella said as she leaned against her husband.

"Psychic now, are you?"

"Why haven't I gotten pregnant again, David? We try enough," she said. He could see a tear forming in her eye and quickly kissed it away. They dropped the blanket in the midst of the foundation and the kiss on her cheek moved to her lips. The kiss deepened and they soon were sitting on the blanket lost in the love and the passion of the moment.

"Well, we haven't gone back and tried it in the back of that pickup again," he laughed.

"We sold that truck to get you one more reliable for your tools. I cried."

"I didn't know that, sweetheart. It was just a truck," he said, petting her hair. His fingers moved to the buttons on the front of her housedress.

"Don't be careless, hon," she said, slowing him down. "I just made this dress."

"You could support us all with your sewing," he laughed. He moved so he could use both hands to gently unbutton the dress. "I think maybe you simply haven't been excited enough to get pregnant. Remember how nervous we were that first time?"

"I thought I'd peed myself," she giggled. "And when I felt you for the first time, I just knew it wouldn't fit."

"You're stretchy. I don't remember any problem with it fitting."

"It hurt a little at first. But then I was so overwhelmed by the sensations my body felt that I couldn't think about the pain."

"Still, there's something to be said for new and what it does to our bodies."

"You want a new wife?" she pouted. She tried to pull her dress closed, but he pulled it down over her shoulders and she relaxed. He unfastened her bra and it, too, fell to the side.

"No, I want this wife in new ways."

"What ways?"

"Well, look around you. I think you have some of that adventurous spirit, too. You put our blanket down right in the middle of the dining room," he laughed. She looked around.

"We can't even tell one room from another yet. We're lying on the grass."

"Just imagine," he said as he moved lower to pull her panties down. "The kitchen is just beyond your head there. Off to your left is the arch that will lead into the living room. Grandmother Abrams' china hutch will be against the wall next to the window there on your right. And you know that big oak table we picked up at the auction last year and stored in the barn?"

"I know the table," she whispered. "We need to refinish it."

"And when we do, it's going to sit in the middle of the dining room right under where you are lying now."

"Oh! David, do you mean I'm naked on the dining room table?" The very thought of it caused a flush to spread from her cheeks down to her tight little nipples.

"Yes, that's right," he whispered. "And I've just gotten home from work. I'm a starving man. I sit at the table to eat my dinner." With that he dipped his head between her legs and licked through her hair.

"David! What are you doing?"

"I'm getting ready to taste my dinner. I've wanted to do this for years. I'm starving, Ella. Let me eat." He pushed her legs farther apart and applied his thumbs to part her nether lips. Almost four years of marriage and it was the first time he'd had his face between her legs — the first time he could see the juices running from her vagina, begging him to taste them.

"It's not clean down there," Ella protested. She pushed at his head but he was insistent. When his tongue touched her opening, her resistance faded. His next lick brought a moan from her lips. He slid his hands down to cup her buns as he pulled her more firmly into his mouth. Once tasting her, he knew he would feast here often. Ella's passion rose quickly and the little glen where their new home would be built echoed with her orgasm.

David crawled up between her legs and nudged her open with his cock. Ella gasped another climax as he slid into her.

"How? Where did you ever learn such a thing?" she gasped.

"I was in the army."

"And you played around even while writing me those lovely letters?"

"Never think that my love. Guys all thrown into the same barracks talk and late at night some of them talk more than they should about things I'd never tell a soul. But it was instructional. And I wanted you at the peak of passion if we are going to conceive our daughter tonight."

"Yes, David! I love you so much. Make me a mommy again. Give me our little girl."

He did his best repeatedly for the next two hours and again when they got home and went to bed. It just didn't take.

"I'M SO SORRY I couldn't give you the little girl that you wanted," he sighed. He sat on the porch smoothing the chunk of wood with the edge of his knife. Thin peels of wood curled away from the blade. Every few cuts he stopped to caress the groove he'd shaped in the wood.

Don't you dare put your tongue on that.

"I know the difference between poplar and pussy."

But do you know the difference between parsley and pussy?

He chuckled deep in his throat letting his finger continue to touch the groove.

"Yes. No one eats parsley."

It's getting too cold to sit out here on the porch at night.

"Are you cold, sweetheart? Let's go in and sit by the fire."

He stood and moved to the door. Pausing he turned to pick up the wood again and carry it inside with him.

Can't stop touching me, can you?

"Never could. And anything that can be done outdoors can be done indoors."

As you showed me when we finally moved in.

"ISN'T HE LOVELY?" she said as they stood in the doorway watching their son sleep. He'd been so excited about moving into his own new bedroom in the home that David built that he could hardly settle to sleep. But now he was out like a light.

"Our precious son looks so much like his mother he couldn't help but be lovely," he said. He put his arms around her and pulled her against his chest. He cupped her breasts and began kissing her neck.

"Mmm. David, we're standing in the doorway to our son's room. Don't do that." She made no effort to remove his hand from her breast, nor to stop him from lifting her skirt with his other hand.

"I think we might not have found the right place yet to conceive our little girl." He continued to nibble on her neck while he worked her panties down. Well, the front of her skirt would hide anything if their son woke up. She felt him prodding at her with his cock and thrust her butt back toward him to make his entry easier. David slid into her waiting vagina.

"We... we shouldn't... be doing this in the hallway," she panted as she pushed back to get him further inside. "We should do this in bed." He unfastened the buttons on her dress and slipped inside to cup her bare breast.

"Believe me, I think that is a wonderful idea," he gasped in her ear. "We'll do that as soon as we finish here."

"How will we know which location we conceived in?"

"We'll probably have to repeat all the places again when we're ready for the next one."

"Next one? David, do you want more than two children?"

"My love, as many as you want."

They groaned as she clamped down on his spurting cock, no longer aware of their sleeping son. They didn't make it all the way to the bedroom for the second time, finding a new position in the shower. Finally, they tried two more positions in bed, crying out their passion with each climax.

IT JUST NEVER happened.

"Not for lack of trying."

It's just that after...

"I know. We waited too long."

I regret every moment of those years after he died. We still had each other. Why didn't we still try?

"It felt like we were trying to replace him. I just couldn't."

Nor could I. David, I hurt you terribly. I'm so sorry.

IT HAD BEEN six months. No, seven. Their precious son, eight years old, rode his bicycle to Papaw and Memaw's house after school. He was so excited to be in third grade. He carried a shoebox under his arm—the diorama of Thanksgiving he'd made in school—wobbling awkwardly as he steered his bike one-handed. The man who hit him said the bike had suddenly swerved out into the middle of the road. No charges were filed.

But their son was still dead.

Parents should not have to outlive their children.

Seven months later, spring was in the air. They'd mourned all winter. David felt the need to be close to his wife like they had been. They'd shared everything. They weren't yet thirty and had so much to look forward to. He reached for her in bed and pulled her close to him. He kissed her gently. She responded, seeming to want the closeness as much as he did. Their kiss deepened and he caressed her breasts through the thin nightgown. He went slowly, giving her as much time to warm up as he could before moving his hand down to the hem of her gown and sliding it up her leg. Her breathing speeded up, became shallower. He touched the soft curls of her pussy but before he could part her lips, her breathing broke into a sob. Her legs clamped tightly together and she rolled away from him.

"Ella..."

"I'm sorry, David. I know you try hard but I'm just not interested. I'm sorry. I love you."

He was stunned. Crushed. Hurt beyond anything he could imagine. First his son. Now... He turned on his side, facing away from her. Silent tears fell from his eyes. Not interested? In him?

HOW DID YOU ever survive? I was so broken. I was driving you away.

"You saved it. It took me a while to realize it, but you saved it."

How?

The wind whistled outside the cabin door and snow had already drifted against the house. Fifty-one years and seventeen days since his son was killed. How had they survived? Why had he kept trying? He put another log on the fire and wondered for the hundredth time if he'd put in enough wood for the winter.

"Your last words. You showed that it wasn't me you weren't interested in. You said you loved me. Without those last three words, we wouldn't have made it."

Just because I said 'I love you?'

"It let me know that there was hope that I could interest you again. You weren't rejecting me. And eventually we thawed the ice between your legs."

More than a year later. Why did I have to wait so long?

"Perhaps because you knew I would wait."

But you wouldn't.

The curve of the wood shaped by his knife was like the flip of her hair on that summer night. She hadn't consciously been growing it out, but she hadn't had it cut since their child died. He always loved her hair. If he closed his eyes he could feel each strand of it as he petted her head. Each hair whittled into the diminishing block of wood.

THEY'D BEEN CONVINCED to join the young marrieds group at the church and tonight was their summer barbecue and bonfire. Ella was self-conscious, thinking they weren't that young anymore. They needed a thirty-somethings group. It was just another thing in her life that she felt disconnected from. They went to the same church they had attended as children. But the familiar faces that they'd always known felt somehow like strangers. Even her husband felt distant, but of course, that was her fault. She couldn't imagine why he stayed with her. She knew for a fact that Dotty Felton had been making eyes at him. She wouldn't be surprised if she lost David to the younger, aggressive woman. Why did she feel so dead? Buried with her son.

They'd eaten, sung some songs, and were getting ready to listen to some storyteller who was the official entertainment for the evening. Darkness had fallen and she slipped back away from the fire into the shadows of the surrounding trees near the stream. She'd heard this storyteller sometimes asked for volunteers and she didn't want to be in his line of sight. She looked across the fire and tried to see David. It was a force of habit. No matter how far away she tried to push him, her eyes were still drawn to him—seeking him out as if he were an anchor. If ever she lost that thin connection she would be adrift and would be lost at sea.

Where was he? She felt a bit anxious as she looked at the crowd. Was that…? No. How could she mistake Bill Crawford for David? No. Was anyone else missing? Had he slipped away with another man's wife because his was too cold and unwelcoming? It had become a habit to push him away. It wasn't even true that she wasn't interested anymore. But whenever he tried to engage her, she pushed him away. Where was he? Her lip began to quiver as she looked at the gathered couples, most sitting close together now as the storyteller got wound up. Her heart rose in her throat as she neared panic. Perhaps he had left—left her to her own cold devices.

Her scream was cut off by the hand clamped across her mouth. Where had he come from?

"You don't want to draw attention to the fact that we are hiding in the shadows," he said.

"David…"

"Quiet. Someone will look and see us. You know you aren't really hidden. They just happen to be looking the other way," he said. "If you make noise, they'll turn and see us."

"See us what?" she whispered. She would never live down the teasing or the reputation if they saw her sneaking away with her husband during a gathering. Even if nothing was happening.

But something was happening. She'd worn jeans and a t-shirt tonight like most of the other women. It was a hot, midsummer night. David's hand was crawling up her belly under the shirt. She felt his hand on her breasts, mauling them.

"David..."

"Hush."

"But..." He spun her around to face him and planted his lips on hers, pushing, forcing her lips to part with his tongue, pinning her against the rugged oak behind her as he worked on her pants zipper. She pushed at his hands but they caught in her waistband and he dragged her jeans and underwear down until he could hook them with his knee and keep pushing while he cupped her ass in his palms. "Don't... We'll..."

"It's been long enough, Ella. Our marriage is on the line now."

"I'll scream."

"Everyone will turn and look at you with your pants around your ankles and your husband's hand on your ass. They'll think you had an orgasm. I'm sure the Millers will have something to say about that. At church Sunday."

"But David..."

"Feel this?" he asked. He pressed his bare cock against his belly as she felt her bra unfasten, releasing her breasts. "Every time I look at you, I'm ready. Whenever I can't see you, I'm ready. Whenever I catch your scent in the air, I'm ready. And you are, too, Ella."

She couldn't deny what his fingers had found as he pried her legs apart and cupped her wet cunt. What was happening? He wasn't asking. He wasn't seducing. He wasn't begging.

He was insisting.

And something inside her gave way. She crushed her mouth against his, grasping his cock in her hand — perhaps less carefully than she might have. He dipped and she moved it to her entrance. He thrust. Hard. He was buried in her and there was no going back. Her husband had claimed her as his own and she opened her knees wider to give him better access. His hands now both cupped her breasts, pinching her nipples as her butt bounced against the rough bark of the tree. His tongue explored deeply in her mouth, cutting off the scream of her first orgasm and muffling the second. Still he pounded at her pussy, pinching and manhandling her breasts, making her come again before she felt him filling her with his seed. He jammed himself into her as far as he could and held himself there as his cock throbbed inside her.

And she wept.

She held him and hugged him and he stroked the long hair that hung past her shoulders as he whispered "I love you."

She pushed at him. Supposing that she was still rejecting him, he slowly pulled away, his cock slipping from her vagina. He looked into her eyes.

"Lie down," she said softly. "I'm going to scrape up your butt now."

He lay down on a bed of old leaves, twigs, and acorns beneath the tree and she mounted him, stroking him upright until she could lodge him again in her pussy. And then it was her turn to insist. She slammed down on him again and again as her tears continued to rain down on his face. She ignored the pain of the acorns under her knees and lifted herself to slam down on him again, reveling in the feel of his cock once again stretching her and filling her. She grabbed at his nipples, pinching and twisting them as violently as he had hers and when she saw him throw his head back and thrust up into her to hold as he came again, she plastered herself against him and sucked his tongue and his moan into her mouth.

This time it was Ella whispering in his ear as they caught their breath. "I love you. I love you, my husband." She fell asleep on top of him, his cock still in her pussy as he petted her hair.

THEIR LOVE-LIFE HAD improved. Not instantly, but steadily. He rocked in his old chair in front of the fire and his knife lovingly shaped the indentation where her spine dipped into her butt. There was not much left of the stick of wood he'd brought into the house last year. Each night he sat and rocked and whittled and remembered.

You don't have to relive this, David.

"I relive it every day. I can't help it."

He pressed his thumb into the small of her back, almost feeling the wood give beneath his pressure.

"DOES THAT HELP?" he asked as he kissed her shoulders.

"Yes. At least that is one place that doesn't hurt. Thank you."

He smoothed his hands lightly up and down her bent back. Arthritis and osteoporosis had bent her back into a painful arch, but it was the cancer that made her suffer. His old hands pushed and rubbed her back, but there was little relief. Hospice was a bitch. If she took enough of the drugs to ease all the pain, she wasn't there at all. She asked for an hour each night to be as clear as possible before she was drugged again.

"I love you, my darling El."

"I love you, D. It won't be long now and I won't have this pain. Don't cry too long. You are still young and strong."

"I'm not young, El. I'm two years older than you."

"But you are strong and you feel young to me. When I'm gone, you could still go out and get a new wife. You don't need to wait. Go out and look up Dotty Felton. She always had the hots for you."

"Dotty died five, six years ago. You know that," he sighed.

"She just wasn't in it for the long haul. Couldn't wait."

"She was happily married and had six kids and a passle of grandkids. That flirtation was just her trying out her wings."

"Did you... Did you ever succumb to her wiles, David?"

"There's never been anyone but you, Ella."

"Even in the dark times after...?"

"No one but you, my love."

"Well, me and that old pair of sweat socks. It took me forever to figure out why those socks always got so crusty." The
old couple laughed softly until Ella gasped for breath.

"Do you need your pill now, my love?"

"In a minute. David, I've loved you for seventy-five years."

"You are only seventy-four years old, dear."

"I loved you before I was born. I will love you long after I'm
dead. I... I can't take the pain anymore, David. Give me my pill.
Please." He held her as she swallowed the pill and drank her
water. He held her as she went off to sleep whispering, "I love
you." He held her as she slipped away late that night.

And since that night, he'd held her in his thoughts. Always.

IT'S COLD, DAVID. Put more wood on the fire.

He absently tossed another log into the firebox. The long
thin twig he still whittled was little more than a finger. He held
it in his hand, just has he'd held her fingers in his hand through-
out the years. Tears fell freely, now.

Look. It's midnight. Merry Christmas, David.

"Ella, I can't go on. I thought it would get better with time,
but it hasn't."

Are you ready, David? Are you truly ready?

"Every time I think of you, I'm ready. Whenever I don't
think of you, I'm ready. Whenever I breathe, I catch your scent
in the air, and I'm ready."

*And I am, too. Toss that stick you're holding in the fire, David.
Take my hand instead.*

"Will you take me with you, Ella?"

*Why do you think I've been hanging around all this time? Come
to me, beloved. It's time to go.*

David closed his eyes, feeling the smooth texture of the
whittled wood in his hand. He smiled and tossed it toward

the fire, not knowing and not caring whether it made it to the flames. His old Buck knife fell to the floor.

His hand, instead, took his beloved wife's and he followed her.

I've known people involved in Renaissance Fairs since the phenomenon began some forty or fifty years ago. I always loved going to them and making up stories about the people, characters, and exhibitors I saw there. The first fair I went to was in Shakopee, Minnesota, sometime in the seventies. The idea brewed in my mind for forty years until I came up with the village blacksmith and the potter. What better names for them than Smith and Potter?

IRON ALCHEMY

I LIKE the heat. Not the mosquito-ridden heat of a humid Minnesota summer. Not the dead dry heat of the Mojave. Not the figurative heat of scholastic demands. Not the adrenalin-inducing heat of walking the beams a hundred feet above the ground.

I know *heat*.

I like the heat of the forge. The heat of iron lying on the anvil awaiting the hammer's kiss. The heat of a welding torch in gloved hands running a smooth bead down an undetectable join. I like the heat that makes sweat run down my back and under my arms. The heat that mosquitoes avoid.

I like the heat.

My great-great-great grandfather, his father, and generations before were blacksmiths. He had a smithy on Marquette Avenue in Minneapolis before he moved out to Stillwater. I wish he'd kept that property and I'd inherited it. That's where they built the Federal Reserve Bank a hundred years later. Today, as impressive as the building is, it's just offices. The Feds gave it up when they realized how expensive it would be to do asbestos abatement and correct the construction flaws. They didn't tear it down, though.

Great-great grandpa didn't like the cold or the mosquitoes, so he moved our family to the California desert where, two generations later, my Dad worked for an ornamental iron company. In sales. Dad likes air conditioning. I got to hang out around the plant when I was younger and spent my summers during high school working there.

That's where I learned to love the heat.

The first job I was assigned at sixteen was on the dock. Young. Healthy. Strong. Lift iron. Flatbed trucks delivered everything from sheet and plate metal to pipes and rods to bars. We call it iron, but in reality, the company deals with just about anything metal. I unloaded it and transported it into the warehouse. I stacked it. I unstacked it and moved it to the shop floor. Repeat. Most of the heavy work is done with forklifts, but sixteen-year-olds aren't allowed to operate a forklift. Sixteen-year-olds lift pieces, secure ropes, operate block and tackle, and do anything where actual manual labor is involved.

Iron, transported on a flatbed truck through the desert in summer, gets hot. My first scar—the one across my right triceps—was acquired when I leaned against an iron bar on the truck. Hot enough to blister, right through my shirt. I learned, though. I learned to love the hot metal. I breathed in the smells of the shop and could tell the difference between grades of iron and sheet metal by scent. I could tell which welder was being used by the smell of heat.

My senior year in high school, I started career development. I went to two high school classes in the morning, then went to my apprenticeship. It might sound medieval, but I had to sign an indenture agreement with the Joint Apprenticeship Committee of the International Association of Bridge, Structural, Ornamental, and Reinforcing Iron Workers.

Five years later I was a journeyman iron worker and I loved the heat.

It's like karma, then, that I moved back to my ancestor's old stomping ground to go to an art school in Minneapolis.

"GRANT, WE NEED that stair railing by end of day. The contractor will be here at five o'clock sharp to pick it up."

PYGMALION REVISITED

"It's finished, Mr. Olson," I answered. It was three o'clock and I'd just stopped to have a Coke before I started on the next job on the list.

"It's what?" my boss yelled. I'd only been working at St. Paul Art Iron for ten days. I didn't think there'd been any problems that would cause him to blow up with me. Even as a journeyman, there's a thirty-day probation period before a worker is protected under the union contract. "Where is it? I haven't inspected your work."

"It's on my bench, sir."

Olson walked over to the bench and began minutely examining every weld in the twisted iron. He grabbed the blueprint and calipers and started measuring distances, angles, and variance. He gripped one of the uprights and tried to shake my weld loose. I think he was looking for any excuse to write me up. It's part of probation.

I was working so I wouldn't have more than a couple million in college loans to pay back. It's stupidly expensive and I intentionally ignored how much debt I was really piling up. It was easy to transfer my credentials from Local 741 in California. That gave me a pretty good hourly wage and benefits once the probationary period was over. I figured one day I'd cash in my pension to pay my college debt.

Olson approved my work and that's how I spent the next four years. I worked second shift and attended Art College during the day. I made wrought iron fences, railings, gates, and decorations. I did window glazing. I did plasma cutting. If it could be done on a bench with a welding torch, plasma cutter, or anvil, it was my job.

My pleasure was firing up the forge and making art.

I MANAGED TO get a studio apartment in what had once been a run-down drug-infested ghetto that was 'restored' to its former glory in the '70s. Forty years later it was a not quite as run-down but almost as drug-infested a ghetto as it had been before the big rescue. The studio I got was in a building that had started out as a residence hotel in the '30s and had some great Art Deco ironwork that had survived deterioration and renovation alike.

My apartment was on the corner and looked out over a little park. You didn't want to walk through it at night. I was pretty content there because I stayed in that apartment for six years. That's when this story really starts. I was doing my studio preparation for my MFA. There aren't very many MFA candidates in sculpture. Well, there aren't that many MFA candidates at all. It's rigorous qualifying and they only take people who already have a BFA. If you made the mistake in your undergrad work in getting a BA, you were considered an academic and not a serious artist. At the same time there were various teaching assistantships available for just about every MFA candidate in the school. But we were there to get started on our careers as 'professional' artists.

What is that, anyway? I can tell you right away that the terms professional and amateur don't have anything to do with the quality of the work produced. Most places, it just means you get paid for *creating* art instead of for *teaching* it.

In four years of undergraduate study, I'd managed to acquire some equipment for my own studio. I knew for a fact that I wasn't going to have a college studio to work in for the rest of my life because I was not interested in teaching. Eventually, I was going to get my own studio. I used my job at Art Iron to get discounted materials, but what I really wanted was to have my own ironworks studio. I had already acquired a welding outfit that the company was retiring. There was nothing particularly wrong with the equipment that a little refurbishing wouldn't cure. It simply wasn't made for the volume of work they were getting. I was the beneficiary.

The real problem was a forge. I had visions of myself working under a spreading chestnut tree. In reality, it would probably be a garage I rented, assuming I could find someone who didn't mind the smell of an iron forge and the sound of hammer and anvil in their back yard. There were lots of portable forges available, but one look would tell you they weren't for a serious smith. They rose on spindly legs to a pot that would be hard to keep lit, even with the electric fans that most came with. I'd still need a pretty significant stand to anchor an anvil to unless I wanted to work on my knees. No.

I SAT IN the line of cars and trucks waiting to enter the grounds at Shakopee. Crews were working on the more permanent structures that would house vendors of everything from roast turkey legs to clothing to magic amulets. I could hear the pounding of a construction crew putting up one of the many stages as I checked in and a guy in a leather vest and blue jeans with a sword at his belt walked ahead of me to the spot where I would set up my smithy.

Six weeks of fun, playing the part of the village blacksmith at the Minnesota Renaissance Festival. They were getting everything set up a week before the festival opened. Even though there were power tools and a couple big gas generators cranking out megawatts, most of the people had already donned some portion of their costumes. Hats, leather aprons, and swords were common. I followed my guide to my spot and backed the trailer into position.

I'd spent every spare minute of the past three months building this. It started with a decent trailer frame that I picked up through *Auto Trader*. Some guy intended to build his own travel trailer and had only gotten as far as stripping the old trailer off the frame before his wife put up an ultimatum. For some reason he chose to keep her instead of his pet project. It was a twelve-foot frame with dual axles and decent suspension. Other than that, nothing but the hitch. As soon as I had it in position, I unhitched and took the truck to the campsite.

The cast campground was not as organized as the festival grounds. Someone had whitewashed crooked lanes around the grounds and marked them with yellow flags. You couldn't park in the lanes. Anywhere else was open with no designated parking or camping spots. There were a few trailers and a few campers, but mostly there were cars and trucks parked as close to the lane as they could get with a tent set up behind. Really! These people had no idea how hard the ground was going to get. For safety, there were power poles with lights scattered through the grounds. I backed up to one and checked the power box. There were all-weather outlets on the pole. Mostly, people would use them to recharge their phones. I wasn't sure what good that would do as there were only half a dozen spots on the entire festival grounds where there was any kind of cell signal. I plugged in my camper. That was all there was to setting up my campsite.

Setting up my blacksmith shop was harder and took until noon the next day. When packed up, the trailer was no higher than the back of the pickup. The truck weighs about 4,500 pounds. The loaded trailer was close to 6,000. Being a black-smith is not only hot, it's heavy. The weight included fold-up sides and back, a roof with extended awning, a built-in forge, the front table with display stock and the anvil. It included the bellows, the coal, and the unformed iron and sheet metal. Off the back of the shop, I had my acetylene welding bench. I'd keep that closed during show hours, but if I needed more stock of artwork, I would have to work late nights.

Finally, I'd cut a spreading chestnut tree, complete with individually cut and hammered leaves and bark that wrapped around the left end of the display. I'd created a leaf form stamp and hammered the leaf veins and texture right into the sheet metal.

Pygmalion Revisited

Under a spreading chestnut tree
The village smithy stands;
The smith, a mighty man is he,
With large and sinewy hands;
And the muscles of his brawny arm
Are strong as iron bands.

His hair is crisp, and black, and long,
His face is like the tan;
His brow is wet with honest sweat,
He earns what'er he can,
And looks the whole world in the face,
For he owes not any man.

Good old Henry Wadsworth Longfellow. The poem was first published in 1840 and I memorized it in the shop when I first learned to use the forge and anvil. Then I went on to learn a bunch of his other poems. They helped set the rhythm for my hammer.

Over the heat of the forge hung a black Dutch oven full of water. It probably wasn't an authentic use of a forge, but I could boil water and keep it going for the twenty minutes that it took me to properly heat the iron. Why did I need boiling water? For chestnuts. I bought a bushel basket of the nuts and each morning I would cut an 'X' in the top of a few dozen. I'd boil a bunch of them two or three times a day and then scoop them out of the water to dry in the little oven under the forge. As each demo concluded, I would open the oven drawer and bring out fresh, hot, roasted chestnuts for the crowd to sample. Even if people are not interested in a demonstration, they'll still stick around to sample a fresh-roasted chestnut.

"OH, MY GOD! What is that horrid stench? Is this going to be here for the entire festival?" a young woman asked. I turned to look at her. The festival opened tomorrow and everyone was practicing their spiels and crafts as the other craftspeople and actors wandered around getting a feel for what would be happening. Once the festival started, I wouldn't really be able to leave my station for more than bathroom breaks and food during the long days. I'd need to be firing up the forge by eight in the morning, and I wouldn't leave it until it was cool, around twelve hours later.

The woman who was standing in front of my shop was attractive, I suppose. She wasn't nearly as exposed as some of the characters were. She wore an apron and a long skirt. Her blouse was buttoned up. The clothes most of the wenches who wandered around the grounds wore were designed to make the most of their assets. I would hardly call the amount of cleavage that was on display an authentic representation of the Renaissance. Most women who dressed like that would be spending their lives on their backs in the sixteenth century. This one, though, looked respectable. She'd already adopted her English accent. That seemed to be a necessity for most characters.

"Are you inquiring about the forge?" I said.

"It stinks!"

"Oh. I hardly notice except first thing in the morning. It's coal in the forge and hot iron on the anvil. Would you like to watch?" I asked. There was no sense rising to the bait of having a smelly exhibit. I was sure there would be others at the festival who would also think it was smelly.

"No. I want you to move. I'm downwind." She pointed at a colorful tent filled with pottery about twenty feet away. It hadn't been there yesterday when I was out helping other vendors get set up.

"What are you doing clear out here?" I asked. "I thought they were making the smithy the last spot on the street." It wasn't a bad spot as there was a stage across from us that would attract people down this alley, but I was sure they put me out here because of the forge and the clanging of my hammer. I'd already been told that I'd have to not hammer during the twenty-minute show times.

"This is where they put me. It was the only spot left," she complained. "This is going to be such a waste."

"I'm Grant Smith," I said, holding out my hand to shake. She looked it over before she accepted the handshake.

"Celia Potter," she said. "Your hands are soft." She pulled back her hand in surprise.

"I don't work without gloves," I said. "I want to work with iron, not become iron. And your hands are soft, as well."

"Clay is damp. It's like playing in mud all day. As long as I keep moisturizing, they don't get dried out." She sighed. "I guess I'm stuck with it. I suppose you'll be noisy, too."

"Not during the show times. That's when I'll be taking my breaks. You can probably continue since pottery is a quiet profession," I ventured.

"It is if I'm throwing pots," she laughed. "It can get noisy, though, if I actually throw them." She was practicing her lines. All of us had humorous little bits that we added in our patter to keep the audience entertained.

"Well, Miss Celia Potter, let me give you a little gift for your lovely soft hands." I reached for my tongs and grabbed a horseshoe nail. It only took a few seconds in the forge for the nail to glow. I set it on the point of my anvil and hammered it gently into shape. When I was satisfied, I dipped it into the water bucket beside the anvil and it hissed. "What size ring do you wear?" I asked.

"A seven," she responded automatically. Men usually have no idea what size their rings are. I've never met a woman who didn't know exactly. I pulled out my sizing rod and slid the horseshoe ring over it. I adjusted the collapsible size until it fit and asked for her hand. She held it out and I slipped the ring on her finger.

"I think this means we're married," I said. "My camper is by the third light pole. You can move in tonight."

"In your dreams!" she laughed. She looked at the ring. "How many other wenches do you plan to marry this week?"

"As many as possible."

I DID A few more demonstrations that morning and handed out some more horseshoe nail rings. One particularly buxom girl gave me a kiss that I know left a lipstick smear on my cheek. I gave her a ring.

"Now you can tell people you got nailed by the village blacksmith," I whispered to her. She giggled and ran off to kiss another guy and leave lipstick on his cheek. Such is the life of the Kissing Wench.

I walked around the fairgrounds and stopped to look over a display of knives and swords. I could hammer out a blade, but they were strictly utilitarian. I wasn't refining steel and didn't much like to work with the harder metal. I always liked to look at good ones, though. A lot of cleavage attached to a very nice-looking girl was pushed over the top of the display case as she leaned in toward me.

"If you see anything you want to touch, just point at it and I'll whip it out for you," she said saucily. Looking down her front, I was pretty sure she had an innie navel. I pointed to her left breast.

"This one seems to have a nice hard point on it," I said. "Of course, I'd want to compare it to the other to make sure I had the best at the Faire." She giggled.

"You're a quick one. How long is your sword?"

"Whatever it lacks in length, it makes up in girth," I said. "I need a nice tight sheath for it." I finally looked up from her breasts and into her eyes. I just held her eyes for a second. She'd need practice at this game if she was going to blush every time a customer fed lines back to her.

"I might have a sheath that would fit," she breathed at last.

"Do you have a tent?"

"One with a single pole, but I sleep in a camper," I answered.

"A bed?"

"Of course."

"I'll fix dinner at my place if we can... sleep at yours."

"Time and place?"

"Eight o'clock. My tent has the flag of Princess Aurora flying in front of it."

"Which one is she?"

"The blonde one, of course."

"Aren't they all blonde?" What did I know about Disney princesses?

"You'll get toad stew for dinner and no sheath if you continue that. There hasn't been a blonde princess since Sleeping Beauty."

"Sleeping Beauty? Now I know who you are talking about. I hope I get to watch her sleep tonight."

I DID. AURORA, who never would tell me her real name, fixed a nice meal over her gas stove and grill—chicken breast, rice, salad. Simple, but good. When we'd cleaned up and went to the camper, she was a lively participant, but made it clear that she was only interested in oral satisfaction. As soon as she felt we'd pleasured each other enough, she pulled underwear and a t-shirt on so there wouldn't be any accidents during the night.

Still, it was nice to sleep cuddled up behind a soft and pleasant girl. Just because she wore a t-shirt to bed didn't mean my hand couldn't be under it. And panties were only a defense against my cock, not my fingers. In the morning, she stroked me off as I fingered her, and she gave me our first kiss before she pulled her shorts on and ran to her tent. Turned out it was our last kiss, too.

OPENING DAY WAS busy and crowded. I had the forge going all day and in addition to horseshoe nail rings that I sold for $5.00, I also had punches that I could use to strike initials and short names into a horseshoe or a blank disk. The horseshoes and blank disks were also $5.00 plus fifty cents per strike.

I also had bronze disks, and even though the raw material was about eighty-five cents a square inch, I could charge $10.00 for a custom stamped one-inch coin. It was a cold stamp process and I had a special clamp to hold the coin to the anvil. On the bottom was my Iron Alchemy logo with no words. It's pretty cool—just a circle with an arrow pointing up to the right. I had a dozen different stamps in addition to the fancy script letters that were always popular. I placed the blank apparatus on the anvil and used a five pound hammer to make the strike. People loved to watch it and then take their freshly minted coin from me.

But by far and away, the most popular thing was to get nailed by the village blacksmith.

By the end of the day, I was exhausted and hoarse. And I'd burned an entire tray of chestnuts. Six weeks of this was going to be more than my voice could take. And, of course, while I was hammering a ring or horseshoe, or stamping a disk, I wasn't selling other merchandise. I sold a lot of little crap during the day, but no artwork. Selling any one of my metal sculptures would have given me more money than the entire take on trinkets. When I got back to my truck that night, I ate a cold sandwich with some chips and drank a beer. Then I fell into bed.

I DEBATED PULLING out Sunday night like a lot of people were, but decided that I'd rather stay in the camper another night than fight the traffic. I was looking forward to getting back to my apartment and a hot shower in the morning, though. I looked in my little refrigerator and pulled out the last steak and some rather droopy asparagus. I lit my grill and threw it all on at once.

"A real gourmet, I see," Celia said as she came up to me.

"Hey, Miss Potter. Are you staying the night?" I asked.

"I'm staying the week. I have too much stock in there to walk away and assume security will just take care of everything. Besides, I need to fire some more mugs," she said.

"You've got a kiln in there? I didn't see it when I came by."

"It's behind the shop. I didn't want a propane kiln destroying the illusion of the Renaissance."

"It's less of a Renaissance Festival these days than a Steampunk and Pirates Fest," I laughed. "Do you have anything you want to toss on the grill while it's hot?"

"I was coming to ask you that. Do you mind?"

"Not at all."

WE MANAGED A pleasant evening. Celia brought a bottle of wine as well as her grillables.

"I figure that when you are in town this week, you can replenish my wine stock if I share it with you," she said.

"I could just drink beer," I answered.

"Oh, the brawny lad needs his ale. What a waste of good wine!"

"If you are attempting to seduce me, kind words are as good as fine wine," I said.

"Seduce? You? Hah! Married on Thursday morning and betrayed by a strumpet Thursday night. Now the straying husband wants *me* to seduce *him*! I think not." She glared at me. I was frozen. What?

"Uh... Celia. It was... I mean... I didn't..."

"Didn't enjoy your time with Aurora One-Night?" she asked coyly.

"I won't deny that I enjoyed a night with Princess Aurora," I said, "but that doesn't mean we're lovers."

"Very well, then. I accept," she said.

"You… Accept what?"

"Your offer of more wine, thank you. I never could hold a grudge."

"You are more of a tease than Aurora One-Night and the Kissing Wench combined," I sighed, pouring more wine.

"So why are you leaving our little piece of paradise?" she asked.

"Well, my gear all has chains and padlocks," I said. "I need to replenish some supplies, dump my tanks, and find an assistant."

"What tanks?"

"Waste water."

"Eww, gross. And why an assistant?" she asked.

"I discovered that it is difficult to keep the demonstration going while still trying to sell goods. There's just too much to keep track of," I admitted.

"That's why I don't really make anything when I'm sitting at the wheel. Everything I throw is immediately cut and reshaped. If someone wants something, I just stop what I'm doing and conduct the transaction."

"Very smart of you. I guess I just had too high an expectation of what I could do while I was here. I actually thought I'd do some serious smithing instead of just trinkets during demos," I said.

"It probably won't be as busy next weekend."

"Labor Day. Four days instead of three and bigger crowds."

"Oh. I forget American holidays."

"You're not American?" I asked. "I wondered how you got such a consistent accent."

"I didn't have to learn it. I was born with it." We sat in lawn chairs and sipped our wine.

"I've an idea. How much did you plan to pay your shill?"

"Hmm. Cast members work for tips. But she won't really be able to get tips because she'll be selling. I think \$75–\$100 a day would be about right. After all, it is fun. And I'd provide food," I said.

"And a bed?" she giggled.

"Oh shit! I'll have to get a tent," I said. I couldn't really expect someone to come out to the grounds in the morning and leave at night. The traffic out was terrible.

"What? She doesn't get treated as well as the princess?" I blushed. Celia laughed. "I have an idea. My friend Leslie Cravens was here today, moaning about how she'd gotten back too late this summer to audition for a cast role. Hire her and she can sleep with me."

"I'm not sure I like the sound of my wife sleeping with another woman," I said.

"It's most men's fantasy," she teased. "Just imagine what might be going on in our tent late at night."

"Most men would rather be present."

"Master Smith! A ring is the only way you will nail either of us."

LESLIE CRAVENS WAS everything I could have wanted except a bedmate. She was a cute blonde grad student in theater at the University. Great at improv, she also had a clear and ringing voice that carried without being harsh or shouted. She quickly adapted some of my lines and interacted well with me during the demos. When I returned to the park on Wednesday, she came with me and immediately tossed her bag in Celia's tent. I arranged credentials for her and we spent that afternoon and all day Thursday rehearsing.

In addition to adapting my lines, she added a number of her own as Friday progressed, often pointing out the fine art I was displaying. People were showing much more interest in it than they had the previous weekend. In the evening, I was the designated cook. Though Celia contributed to the food more than I thought necessary, I grilled something every night. And we shared a bottle of wine and a lot of flirtation each evening before Celia and Leslie retired to their tent.

"You know, if you were making swords and armor instead of metal birds, you'd sell a lot more of the expensive items," Leslie said.

"Unfortunately, they don't teach sword-making and armory to union apprentices," I said. "I don't want to work with steel for swords. It is a long and arduous process."

"Arduous! Listen to that vocabulary, Leslie," Celia exclaimed. "Master Smith is educated with more than his hammer and tongs. Hammer and tongue, perhaps!"

"Oh, he *does* know how to heat things up," Leslie joined in. "Let us not forget that."

"People rave about his nuts," Celia said.

"All right!" I said. "I shall have to praise your beauty with poetry if you keep this up."

"Oh, please do!" Celia said. I turned to her.

*Fair was she to behold, that maiden of seventeen
    summers.
Black were her eyes as the berry that grows on the thorn
    by the wayside,
Black, yet how softly they gleamed beneath the brown
    shade of her tresses!
Sweet was her breath as the breath of kine that feed in
    the meadows.
When in the harvest heat she bore to the reapers at
    noontide
Flagons of home-brewed ale, ah! Fair in sooth was the
    maiden.*

"Oh, my. Celia, you didn't warn me," Leslie said, faking a swoon. Celia held my eyes and I realized she really did have remarkably dark, almost black, eyes.

"Good evening, Master Smith," Celia finally sighed as she stood. "Thank you for your recitation. We really need to get our rest now."

"And good evening to you, Mistress Potter. And you, Maid Leslie. Until the morrow." I watched the sway of their hips as they walked away, thinking I would like to join them.

Hmm. Armor.

THERE ARE MANY industrial uses for sheet metal. Think about your automobile. A big sheet of metal is laid over a form and a high-pressure mate is stamped down on top of it. *Voilà!* A car door. A hood. A grille. A bumper. We used formed sheet metal — usually aluminum — to make window frames for buildings.

But a lot of art is made from sheet metal, as well. Most of it is flat or nearly flat art. Material is embossed, chased, bent. The processes are cold. I like the heat. I like the hammer. I started creating deeply three-dimensional art from sheet metal by using the forge and hammer. That's how I arrived at making birds. I could heat the sheet metal — usually 14 gauge mild steel, just over a sixteenth of an inch thick — and hammer it into the shape I wanted on an anvil. It takes a lot of twisting and turning with the tongs while I hammer on it. Inside curves are easier than outside curves. With the right hammers and enough patience, I could create a bird's body, wings, legs, and head. I had a lot of hammers and a lot of patience. Once the body was created, I stamped out feathers and welded them to the body.

Saturday morning, I was at the forge at seven. My stock included various bits of sheet metal and I chose a sheet of the eighth-inch bronze I used to cold stamp my coins. Most of my stock had been punched for the inch diameter coins, but I had a piece that was 12"x12". Bronze has a much lower melting point than iron—only a little over 1700°. It becomes quite malleable at lower temperatures and hammers well.

By eight-thirty, my hammer rang out as I began shaping the hot metal.

WHEN THE SATURDAY crowd started showing up at eleven, a man's chest had begun to emerge from the sheet. It was all repoussé work, hammered from the inside to create the shape of the outside. Later, I would work on a pitch-covered form that would allow me to chase the shape from the outside of the curve and emboss the front.

Leslie and Celia admired the work when they arrived.

"Les, you aren't showing him enough boob," Celia laughed. "You're so flat-chested in this sculpture." Leslie adjusted her peasant blouse down so it exposed the maximum amount of breast legal for the festival.

"I think it must be yours he's using as a model," she said. "Even the village smith couldn't miss these." And we were right back into our somewhat suggestive banter. Leslie surprised me when she wandered out farther from my stand and began to sing. People began to gather around to listen to her and as they did, she moved ever so slightly up toward the booth. I knew the words and wondered where she'd found the music. "Under a spreading chestnut tree…" When people were near enough, she began talking about the smithy and the work I was doing. At the appropriate time, I joined in the spiel to talk about my tools.

We sold half a dozen rings and three coins. Leslie pointed out the artwork and a couple people stopped to talk about it as I pulled the first batch of roast chestnuts out of the oven and served them to our audience. We were beginning to really click as a team.

BEING WITH LESLIE and Celia was fun. I was really enjoying their company and Leslie and I were working together like a real team. She'd sold two of my higher priced pieces, which would have been enough by themselves to pay for my participation in the show, my expenses, and provide a nice profit. Leslie's voice was clear and enchanting. She'd made up the music for 'The Village Blacksmith'. I was impressed. I was going to give her a nice bonus at the end of the show.

She provided the bonus for me.

"WHERE'S CELIA?" I asked when Leslie came to dinner alone the night before our last day of the festival.

"Um… Not feeling well. You know. Girl problems."

"I should take her something to eat," I said.

"I covered it. What's for dinner, Master Smith? I brought wine."

"I was preparing an entire rack of pork ribs. We might have to refrigerate some."

"Pork ribs? The kind you eat with your fingers?" she asked.

"Well, you can try to eat them with a knife and fork. I think fingers is the better choice."

"Sounds messy. Delightfully messy. We'll have to clean up each other's fingers afterwards."

"I have wet wipes," I laughed.

"How about if I lick yours and you lick mine?" she asked.

That was the start of the flirting. The end was with my cock buried in her to the balls. Unlike Princess Aurora, Leslie had no intentions of stopping short of the main event. It had been a long time since I'd had a girlfriend and I really liked Leslie. In fact, I liked her all night long. Several times.

Devon Layne

"WE'D BETTER FIND showers this morning," she whispered when she'd climaxed again. She gripped my cock with her pussy muscles and I fired off. "I love the way you just keep coming and coming. I'll miss that," she said.

"How about we plan a repeat tonight," I said.

"Um… I'm headed back to town tonight. Classes started this week and I just cut the first week. Sorry I can't stay to help pack up. I've got a ride back as soon as we close tonight."

"Well, I'll call you later in the week," I said.

"Sure."

I REALLY APPRECIATED Leslie's lush curves, though our banter was perhaps a little off on Sunday. The crowd was a little smaller and mostly repeats. Some of the vendors were beginning to pack up their shops by three o'clock.

"Grant," Leslie said after the small crowd disappeared from my last demo. "I want you to meet my boyfriend, Jim. He's working on his MFA in theatrical design. If it's okay with you, we'll leave now and try to only spend an hour in the parking lot." *Her boyfriend? Her what??*

"Sure, Maid Leslie. Let me grab your pay for the weekend," I said.

"Oh, just give it to Celia and she'll get it to me," Leslie said. She leaned into her boyfriend and gave him a serious kiss. Sending me a message. "'Bye!" They took off.

"Fucking hell!" I breathed. I considered closing my shop, but I needed to pound on something. I pulled down the bronze bust I was working on and heated it in the forge.

I PLUNGED THE hot metal into my bucket of water and it was still hissing when Celia spoke. "How about if I go get dinner ready and you clean up now?"

"Don't bother. I'm not hungry," I lied.

"Grant, don't be hard on her."

"Hard on her? Why should I ever be hard again? I fucking hate women!" I practically shouted at her.

"Gee, thanks a lot," she spat back.

"You knew! You even helped her. She's got a boyfriend! Why in five weeks did that little detail not come up?"

"She wanted to flirt and be playful."

"Well, she got it, and a lot more, too. I've never had a one-night stand before in my life, and now I've had two in six weeks. Neither one of which would have happened if I thought there wasn't a chance for a relationship to build. There's no way I'm trusting another woman. Period. End of paragraph. End of story."

Celia stood there with a tear running down her cheek. I didn't care.

"I really underestimated you, Grant. I'm sorry." She left and a few minutes later I saw her car pull up to her booth and she pushed boxes of her remaining stock into the back. Like most of us who had a craft to sell, she had a large vehicle. When the boxes were loaded, she pulled around to the back of her booth where her portable kiln was located.

I sighed. I wasn't much of a gentleman if I didn't go help with the heavy equipment. I stuffed the envelope with Leslie's pay in my pocket and walked over to the Potter's Shed.

"Can I help you move the kiln?" I asked. She spun around and looked at me. There were still tear tracks on her cheeks and the threat of more to come.

"I'm a woman!" she spat.

"It doesn't mean we can't be friends," I said. "I'm just a little sore right now. I'd like to help you if you'll let me."

"Thank you," she said. There was a specific packing order for the pieces and I loaded them in the van as she directed. When it was all packed up, she said, "Thank you, again. It would have been a bitch to get it loaded by myself. I'm headed home. I'll see you around."

"Celia, I… um… I have Leslie's pay envelope. She said to just give it to you. Please tell her the bonus was already figured and set aside before… before last night," I said.

"She'll appreciate that. She really liked working with you, you know. I'm sorry for what happened. I should have known."

"Let's just forget it," I said. "There will be other shows. I'm sure we'll meet again. Good luck."

I watched as she silently got in the van and drove off.

Fuck. Women.

I WAS A week late for classes, too, but I'd gone in last Monday and confirmed my space and met with my advisor. My entire year was guided self-study, meaning that at the end of the year I would present an exhibition of my work for review. Assuming it would pass, I would receive my MFA in May. I had a series of drawings that I'd presented with brief descriptions of each and was approved for my final project. As part of my school benefits, I was given what was loosely referred to as studio space. It amounted to a designated section of a warehouse. A couple dozen 3-D art students who were working on their final exhibitions would be housed there. Another section was a large teaching studio.

Over the summer, I'd discussed my needs for the kind of work I would be doing and was granted an outside wall near the huge garage doors that opened into the space. I would be able to pull my trailer in and set up in almost the same fashion that I used at the festival. The big difference was that I would not have the display section or customer counter set up. Instead, I would have another workbench where I could set up my welding and plasma cutting equipment.

I locked up my trailer and pulled it out of the Ren Faire as all the temporary buildings were being dismantled. There were a few buildings that held kitchen facilities and fair offices that were permanent, but the majority weren't designed to withstand a Minnesota winter. They were essentially stage props. The crews would be working there another week or more to store the pieces.

It took me the rest of the day to set up the trailer in my designated space in the studio and connect the big exhaust fan that would be on anytime I had the forge lit or that I was welding. Basically, anytime I was in the studio. Everything had to pass a safety inspection, and an open charcoal forge was a big red flag to our fire department. And OSHA was very interested. They'd be in the next day to inspect and I couldn't do any work in the studio until afterward. If it weren't for my union credentials, I don't think I would have passed inspection.

I headed for Art Iron to see if they had any work for me.

"OH, MY GOD! What is that stench? Don't tell me!" the voice behind me said in richly accented English. I spun around and nearly dropped the hot plate of metal in the process.

"Celia?"

"At least you aren't burning chestnuts, as well," she said with a roll of her eyes.

"What are you doing here?" I asked stupidly.

"What do you think? I'm working on my MFA project."

"I didn't know you were a student here! In pottery?"

"In clay. I don't just make jugs for your grog. Barbarian!" she scoffed. She stomped off to a studio space some yards away.

Between us were all the 'hot boxes.' My forge was in the slot nearest the door. It wouldn't take too much for me to back the truck in, hook up, and leave. It was tempting. Next to me was the kiln. This wasn't a little portable like Celia's propane kiln. In different compartments, people fired all kinds of things. Mostly, it was for the people who did castings and had to fire their molds.

Then, of course, were the crucible furnaces where metals could be melted and then cast in said molds. There were different furnaces for precious metals—in which a small amount would be melted for casting jewelry—and for larger projects like bronze casting. It was the hot side of the studio and supplemented the heaters during the cold months for the entire space.

The other side of the studio was the cold side. The most common form of 3-D art was the bronze casting. That started out with clay and the artists who worked with it. I wasn't quite sure what Celia meant when she said she worked with clay if it wasn't pottery and it wasn't molds. In the front corner of the studio opposite me were the stone artists and carvers. The studio tended to be a noisy place and everyone in it wore ear protectors. I watched Celia as she moved to her section of the studio and cast one more look at me over her shoulder.

"What a bitch," I mumbled. "Why does she have to be so fucking cute?"

CUTE WAS THE operative word. I liked to look at her. Well, I liked to talk to her when we weren't fighting. Nothing had been quite the same as it was back at the festival. She was about 5'3" and probably didn't weigh as much as my arms. What can I say? Lifting iron, sheet metal, torches, and a hammer all day tended to add bulk to the upper body. I'm six feet tall but weigh 225. A doctor tried to tell me that according to my height and weight, I should lose twenty pounds. Then he did a BMI. He decided that I didn't have any fat to lose and shut up. He got me aware of my overall fitness, though, and I tried to do a lower body workout or aerobic workout every day. I rode my bike to the studio regularly.

Where I had almost black hair that covered my head and chest, Celia's was more a reddish brown—sort of mahogany. And her eyes were so dark you couldn't see the difference between the iris and the pupil. She never wore suggestive cloth-ing, but all the 3-D artists tended to wear clothes that weren't bulky. Celia had a nice shape. More slightly built than Leslie, it was still obvious that she had all the right pieces in the right places. *Cute, damn it.*

I tried not to pay attention to her. I'd sworn off women. And she'd been complicit in getting Leslie in my bed. That still irritated me. Still, when we found ourselves together for a few minutes, the banter was cordial and a little flirtatious at times.

"What are you firing today?" I asked her casually. The kiln was cold for loading. What she was firing would tell me how long the kiln would be in service. She turned toward me and sighed as she pulled off her gloves.

"It's the first batch of porcelains for my project. They were a bitch to form and now I have to wait and watch for three days before I find out if it holds together," she said. She set the tem-perature sequence to heat slowly and wandered over to look at the drawings I was working on. For porcelain, the kiln would heat to about 2,500° over the next 24 to 36 hours, depending on how she was monitoring it. Then it would cool for a day before she could unload it. It was a cold day at the forge and I was working on the designs for the bust I planned to create.

"And here I thought you were a potter," I laughed. The glimpse I'd had of what was going into the kiln showed that these weren't a bunch of coffee mugs.

"That, dear sir, is like calling you a coin stamper or a horse-shoer. We have simple projects we can sell to wide audiences at a low price. Then we have our art."

"What inspired you to work in clay and porcelain?" I asked. "As an artist."

"I love the malleability of the material. I love the feel of the clay in my fingers. It allows me to have my hands in it. Unlike you. You use tools to shape the metal. You can't reach in and bend the hot metal in your fingers," she said.

"I could once, I suppose," I laughed. Yeah. Then I wouldn't have fingers left. "Clay, porcelain, glass — they all seem so temporary. I work in metal, mostly iron and bronze, but some other composites, because I want my art to last for generations. Doesn't it depress you to think that what you create will be broken sometime? That it is fragile?"

"You are showing your ignorance, Grant Smith. Let me ask you this. When they dug up the tomb of Emperor Qin Shi Huang, how many iron soldiers were in his army?" she asked.

"Okay. I admit. They were all terracotta."

"And well over 2,000 years old. How many iron artifacts told of the Greek gods and the culture of classic Greece?"

"I don't think they had too much in the way of iron yet in the era you are asking about. It was mostly bronze until 1,000 years BC."

"How many bronze artifacts were uncovered and used to tell the story of the culture between 3,000 and 1,000 BC?" she persisted.

"Most metal was used for weaponry and industrial purposes. It was recycled when broken and forged into new products," I admitted. "I see where you are going with this."

"Exactly. Most of what we know about ancient cultures is from the pottery they left behind. Not from the metal artifacts. Doesn't it depress you to think that what you heat in your forge and bend with your hammer will one day be melted down to make an iron girder in a skyscraper or bushings for someone's plumbing?" she asked.

"You have a great way of depressing people, Celia."

"How about I buy you a beer to cheer you up," she asked. This was a nice offer out of the blue and I started to pack up. It was Friday, after all, and nearly Christmas. Celia hesitated and ran her finger lightly over the sketch I'd been working on. She sighed but didn't say anything.

THE NEXT TIME we went out for a beer after working at the studio, it was late January. I'd been out the entirety of the holiday break. First I flew to California to see my parents for Christmas. When I got back, Art Iron had a huge Art Nouveau restoration project. I worked on twisting vines and flowers ten hours a day for two weeks straight. I was pleased with the amount of overtime they were willing to pay for the project. I finally got back to the studio and started forming the center-piece to my exhibit—Venus Rising.

That's not an unusual theme for sculpture projects. I knew there were at least two bronze castings and a stone sculpture among the final projects for MFAs. Our ideas of the goddess have been shaped by two artworks. First, is Botticelli's "Birth of Venus" in which the goddess demurely steps from a seashell, covering her important bits with hand and hair. The second is the armless sculpture by Alexandros of Antioch, commonly known as the Venus de Milo, complete with its hard, masculine face.

In my opinion, neither does justice to the beauty or sensuality of the Greek myths. Aphrodite, or Venus, is the goddess of love. In the sculpture, she looks like a shrew at best and a hermaphrodite at worst. She covers her waist in a towel to hide a cock and balls. Okay, that's my opinion. Botticelli shows a demure, shy, embarrassed woman trying to figure out why she is standing naked in a seashell. Scarcely the image of the goddess who boasts of her beauty and stands naked in front of Paris for his judgment, or who bribes him by offering him the most beautiful woman on earth for his wife. We know how that ended up. No, Venus is the very embodiment of sexuality and feminine wiles. She is the great deceiver of men, manipulating them by their balls. Still, she calls and we go to her willingly.

In my hammered bronze sculpture, Venus arises from the sea like a swimmer breaking the surface. One arm is outstretched above her. One hand pushes at the surface of the water to gain more height. Her head is thrown back, water streaming from her hair. Her breasts are proudly thrust up and forward as she emerges from the waves, shouting for joy.

That's all in my mind. I know it will be a bust emerging from the water lapping around her. Hair will stream down in abundance and support the sculpture in its upright position. Only the front of the arms will be shown as the back is hollow — as hollow as her words. And there will be no face. Who can know the face of a woman behind the mask she wears?

"IS THIS THE beginning of the masterwork?" she asked as I doused my charcoal. Granted, it didn't look like much. The piece would be created in pieces that were to be welded together. In places, the hammer marks would be evident as the raw waves from which she emerges. In other places, she will be polished smooth with all trace of the hammer removed. When it comes to her hair, it will be worked with a fine etching tool to high-light every strand. *God! She's beautiful.* Like every man before me, I'd lay down my life for her.

"Not much to look at yet," I said. "This is just the beginning of the water."

"You've been working hard," she said. "It's Friday night. How about a beer?"

"You've lit the kiln. More porcelain?" I asked as I cleaned up.

"Bisque firing so I can work on the glazes. Like iron, it has to be heated more than once."

We headed to a little bar on Nicollet that also happened to serve great Italian food. I'd been working over the forge since ten this morning and hadn't eaten anything.

"Seems like we should have wine tonight," I said. "May I treat?"

"Well, what do you have in mind?" she said with a raised eyebrow.

"I was thinking of the cheapest Chianti on the menu. And I plan to eat a huge helping of their lasagna."

"Chianti is only good if it is cheap. You get the high priced and more highly refined Chiantis and you might as well be drinking a California Cab," she laughed. "I'll have the cannelloni. Have you ever had it?"

"No. I'll trade you bites if you agree."

"Be careful. It's sounding like a date," she said. I stopped and looked at her. If it hadn't been for this fall, I'd definitely have dated her. I changed the subject.

"I didn't know that about Chianti and California Cabs. All this time I thought I liked it because it was cheap."

"In this instance, your barbaric tastes prove refined."

We drank our wine and talked about our projects. Over the break, Celia had a pottery show in St. Cloud. Some holiday festival and she sold a lot of mugs. Most had a rendition of Santa on them. I told her about the Art Nouveau project I'd worked on.

"That must be for the restoration of the Palladium," she said. "It's a shame that all that beautiful metalwork is just going to decorate a chichi shopping mall."

"Is that what they're doing with it? Too bad. It is some beautiful work, but it's craftwork, not art. Most of the original work was stamped out. There was more art in the restoration than the original."

"And what's the difference between art and craft?" she asked. "Don't you think we are too quick to judge what is art? I know I scoffed at the idea that blacksmithing was an art form. And I'll bet you felt the same way about my ceramics."

"I confess to a modicum of truth in that statement. We weren't showing our best side at the festival."

"I certainly wasn't." She lowered her eyes and cut one of the cannelloni in half to put more on my plate. I think I'd already eaten half of her meal. Cannelloni was rising to the top of my favorite foods list.

"Neither was I," I confessed. "I certainly wouldn't have done some of the things I did if I had been."

"Leslie and her boyfriend broke up," Celia said flatly.

"I'm sorry to hear that. They appeared to be very much in love. Of course, appearances can be deceiving," I said. Just a little snide, I admit.

"She asked me to tell you she was available if you'd like to get together."

"I think not. I wouldn't trust myself."

"It's her you don't trust, isn't it?"

"She deceived me and cheated on her boyfriend. Exactly where would trust enter into it?"

"If she had told you she had a boyfriend would you have made love to her anyway?" Celia asked.

"No. I'm not that kind of guy. I really thought we had built something during the five weeks we were working together. I wouldn't have done that if I didn't think she felt... something."

"And then if she came to you and said she'd broken up... Would you have seen her then?"

"Probably," I said. "Yeah. Definitely. I won't lie to you and say I was in love with her when we went to bed, but I saw long term potential there. If we could have rebuilt what we had at the festival, I would have jumped at the chance. More the fool, me."

"And me," she sighed.

"Celia, don't take it personally. I've forgiven you for your part in it and ask you to forgive me for mine," I sighed. "I realized that you and I didn't work together for ten hours a day. The only part of the show we really shared was dinner and wine. I'm sure you got most of your impression of me from my one-night fling with the Princess and whatever Leslie told you. I don't hold it against you."

"Thank you. But you still hate women, don't you?"

"Hate is probably too strong a word. Trust? Just not ready to put it on the line for a woman."

THE NEXT THREE months were intense. This art takes time. I've seen artists who could fling paint at a canvas and have a masterpiece in hours. But heating and hammering, heating and hammering—that takes time. So does shaping, drying, firing, glazing, and firing. Nerves were frayed by the end of April. Some students who were behind were rushing their projects and we had a rare visit by the advising staff to the warehouse when most of us were there. They warned us that we were in a critical phase of our work and that we should continue to work with care and deliberation. They would not remove our studio setups if we didn't meet the all-school exhibition schedule.

It was a relief. These guys understood art, even if they were teachers.

But then I found out the Art Iron project had a phase two and they wanted me to restore a bunch more pieces for the Palladium, which was now properly being called the Palladium Mall. It included creating a couple new pieces as well. I was out for two weeks earning beaucoup bucks, but it wasn't helping my project.

I GOT TO the studio early Monday morning and found Celia in a heap in front of the kiln. She was crying. I rushed to her.

"What is it? Celia, are you all right? Are you hurt?" I said. I put an arm around her and she collapsed against me.

"It exploded. It's ruined. My centerpiece is ruined."

"Oh, my god!" I looked in through the open door of the kiln and saw hundreds of shards of pottery scattered around the inside. "I'm so sorry, Celia. That's so terrible."

"I don't know if I messed up the settings on the kiln or if someone changed them. It was supposed to be a bisque firing and was way too hot. You can't fire moist clay at twenty-two hundred." That wasn't the kind of mistake you'd expect an artist of Celia's level to make. I was shocked at the implication and my eyes automatically went to where my bust had stood for two weeks while I was working. Everything seemed okay, but I would be locking down the front of my wagon from here on out.

"Is there anything in the kiln that is usable?" I asked. She shook her head. "Let's clean it out and leave for the day, then. I've been gone two weeks. Another day won't put me any further behind."

We worked together to clean up the mess and then both made sure our work stations were secure and no artwork was where it could be damaged. Then I held her hand and led her to my truck.

"Where are we going?"

"Just for a drive. I'll show you a couple cool things I've found and treat you to lunch. Did you know my ancestors were from around here?" I asked.

I just wanted to distract her from the problem she had and the only thing I could think of was to show her where my family had worked as blacksmiths. She was amazed at the site on Marquette that's now occupied by what was the Federal Reserve Bank. Then we drove to Stillwater and I showed her the site where he'd moved his shop. We ended with dinner in Hudson, Wisconsin and I drove her home. On the way home, she sat in the middle seat of the truck and held my arm as I drove. She seemed to be studying it as much as holding it for comfort or security.

I walked her to her door and she hugged me. Then looking up into my face she gave me a light kiss and went inside, thanking me for getting her through the day.

IT WAS WHILE I was getting ready for bed that night, thinking of the light touch of her lips on mine, that the answer to her question came to me. I wondered if she'd even remember asking it over three months ago. "And what's the difference between art and craft?" she'd asked.

Except a forge, I used the same materials and tools at my job at Art Iron as I used to create my art in the studio. I was using a plasma cutter to finely cut individual strands of hair in my sculpture. The same as I used one to cut a grille for a security gate. I welded pieces together the same as I welded iron rods in place for the elevator gates. I even used the exact same skills.

Celia used the same clay, firing process, and glazes for coffee mugs as she used for her artwork. But losing an entire kiln full of mugs would not have affected her the way losing her project today had. It wasn't the skill, the material, or the tools. It was what the artist put into the artwork. The soul.

VENUS WAS SHAPING up nicely. In fact, caressing her shape affected me. How can you get turned on by your own artwork? Yet, as I ran my hand over the smooth round breasts and flat stomach to where it would join with the waves, I couldn't help but wish I had a woman as beautiful as this beneath my fingertips.

There was just one detail left and I got hard thinking about it. She needed nipples. I'd worked on a mill at Art Iron to get the exact shape and size. A steel punch. Usually this kind of work was done by a machinist, but we had the necessary equipment. I ran my finger over the surface and the die. I lined the bowl that I would use on the anvil with pitch and heated the bust. Anyone who grabbed that boob at 800° F would regret it. Maybe that's what women needed to prevent unwanted advances. I seated the bust in the bowl and positioned the punch.

"No! Stop, Grant! Please, stop!" I didn't hear it too well, but enough that I glanced up to see Celia practically flying across the studio. I had the hammer back and could still make the impression if I struck, but she looked so frantic. *Damn it!*

I pulled the bust out of the mold and cooled it in the water bucket. It didn't do to ever leave hot metal on the anvil while you were distracted.

"What is it?" I snapped. I'd have to go through the whole process over again. I pulled my ear protectors off.

"Please don't do that," she panted. "It's wrong. It's not… It doesn't… It's just wrong."

"Miss *Potter*," I spat with an emphasis on her profession. "What makes you think you know what is right and wrong about metalwork?"

"I…" she calmed down a little and there was pleading in her eyes that I'd never seen before. *The passion. The soul of the artwork.* "Grant, I know it's difficult, but can you trust me? For ten minutes?" I looked around the studio. Apparently, we were the only ones there. I didn't even know when Celia had shown up. I thought I was alone. Oh well. Today's work was ruined anyway. I was in the wrong space to create what I wanted.

"Okay. Ten minutes. Then I'm going home and getting drunk. What is it?" I was still snappish. Over the past few weeks, we'd developed a good friendship. Ever since I drove her around after the kiln disaster.

"Take off your gloves and apron. I want to blindfold you." She was wearing a scarf and removed it as I took off the gloves and peeled off the silk liners beneath. "So, that's the secret of your soft hands," she said, looking at the silk gloves I wore inside the welding gloves.

"That and butter," I said.

"What?"

"My grandfather taught me that milkfat was the easiest way to keep my hands from turning to leather. Said that's why dairy farmers always had soft hands back in the day when they milked by hand."

"You're full of surprises. Now just get this on and relax. I won't hurt you. Stand right here. Give me a second. Okay."

She positioned me and scuffled around, took my hand, and then pulled it toward her. I felt skin beneath my fingertips. Her left arm was raised above her head and she guided my hand down to her shoulder and on down to her chest. My hand glided over her bare breast. *My god!* She was topless and was guiding my hand in touching her. I could feel the small point of her nipple in the palm of my hand and then between my fingers as she drew it farther onto her stomach until I touched the waistband of her jeans. She pulled my hand back to her arm and started the path down again. I was less startled this time and began to absorb the textures and shapes beneath my fingers. When I reached her waist again, she brought my fingers back to her shoulder and then let me find my own way down her torso. I explored much more thoroughly. And when I reached her nipple, I bent my head and took it between my lips. She sighed.

Could this have been it? Was my subconscious playing tricks on me? Had I really hammered a bronze bust patterned after the woman whose flesh was in my mouth and in my hands?

I continued my blindfolded exploration down her body and this time found no blue jeans at her waist. My fingers wandered down into her pubic hair and into the moist folds of her sex. I continued to suckle on her taut nipple as my fingers explored her folds. Her nipple was smaller than I imagined. Longer. I could feel the outline of her areola with my tongue. No wonder she had stopped me. I had nearly ruined it.

"How did you know?" I asked as I kissed up her chest and onto her neck and chin.

"I know my own body," she whispered. I kissed her. It was the first time other than a peck on the cheek or the one light kiss the night I drove her around my family sites that we had kissed. Her lips were soft and welcomed mine. As I explored the wet folds of her sex, she opened to me fully. Our tongues danced together and I felt her hands at my belt.

"Grant," she whispered.

"Yes, Celia. Yes."

"This isn't for one night. Please tell me. This isn't for one night."

"Yes, Celia. This is for as long as you will have me."

"Then love me, Grant Smith. Love my body and my mind."

"May I look at you, now, Celia? I need to see your eyes," I whispered as she freed my cock. Her hands moved up and released the blindfold. The depth of her coal black eyes drew me and I saw reflected a man starved for love and hopeful for the future.

"I am yours, Grant. I will always be yours."

She leaned back against my worktable and guided my cock to her entrance. She stared into my eyes as I pushed forward and we kissed again.

I fell in love.

That is not true. I realized I had been in love from the moment I heard her voice at the fair. "Oh, my god! What is that horrid stench?" I knew I would hear this voice forever.

CELIA WAS IN my arms that night in my apartment. She was in my arms when I awoke. She was in my arms when we kissed goodnight again. My life had changed. I was no longer alone.

Of course, that didn't mean we were suddenly excused from life. I still had to work at Art Iron. We both still had to finish our exhibitions. We worked hard and I helped her move her things into my apartment. I'd never seen so much pottery!

I did the final cutting and welding of my centerpiece. In a whispered conversation late at night, we decided to hold a joint exhibition. Our advisors agreed. The big day finally came and we began our installation. I set up Venus Rising on a table in the center of the space and was surprised when Celia rolled a cart up next to the same table.

"Are we going to share the centerpiece?" I asked.

"Don't you think that's appropriate? We were each other's models."

"We were... I was what?"

"Did you think I was any more immune to molding you than you were to me?" she asked. "Help me lift this. It is a little heavier than my other pieces." She had been very secretive about her centerpiece after the explosion in the kiln. She kept everything locked up and when it came time to fire it she slipped into the studio late at night and stayed with the work for three days. Each time. It had to be fired for the bisque, and for the glaze, and finally the vitrification. When she unveiled the piece I saw it was a torso of a man. By the shape of the arms, I could tell it was me.

I lifted it onto the table and Celia began moving it around.

"Are we putting them right up tight together?" I asked.

"I hope so. I like it when we're tight together. I like it when you hold me in your arms. I like it when the steel is clay and the porcelain is bronze." I braced my Venus and she slid the porcelain into place. The arm wrapped around the back of the goddess. The right hand was raised and cupped the left breast of my goddess. The figure bent forward slightly and barely touched the other breast, the non-existent faces caught in an invisible kiss. It was a perfect fit.

"What is the title?" I asked.

"Vulcan, of course," she said. She turned to kiss me and I melted in her arms.

Vulcan. The god of fire and volcanos. The god of metalworking and the forge.

The god of heat.

The husband of Venus.

NOTE: *"Mixed Media" was first published in* **Lustily Ever After***, an anthology of rewritten myths and fairy tales with an erotic edge. The anthology is still available at https://www.amazon.com/Lustily-Ever-After/ dp/B01ILEB8CA/ and "Mixed Media" is republished it here by permission. Thank you to Sophia Soror of A Two Dame Production for returning republishing rights to me!*

In this version of the Pygmalion myth, we are asked to consider the story from the perspective of the artwork taking shape beneath the artist's hands. What would happen if it was the artwork that fell in love with the artist rather than the other way around.

MIXED MEDIA

MY **FIRST** awareness was a splash of color—a violent assault on my infant senses. An awakening. It touched every fiber of my latent being with passion, anger, madness.

I was alive.

And then there was nothing.

No. There was, with my awareness of self, an awareness of *other*, as well. I dwelt upon that.

I would like to claim that in my embryonic state, all the mysteries of the universe were revealed. That I transcended the mundane. That I understood the mind of God. But truthfully, those were concepts that had not even dawned on my burgeoning awareness. My mind, my being, was filled with only one thought. There was *other*. I was not alone. All my desire and my being was focused on *other*.

When you have but one thought and it keeps playing over and over, time crawls. How many times can you count to one in an hour? A day? An eternity? And yet I was never bored. I was refreshed with every thought of *other*. Deep within me, I yearned for *other*.

The next stroke was gentler. Or perhaps, since it did not startle me to consciousness, it only seemed gentle. Passion continued to underlie my awareness, but it was tempered with sadness. A sense of great loss overwhelmed me and I desperately clung to the desire for *other*, begging to not have it torn from me. My heart, if I had such a thing, was filled with inconsolable longing for *other*. Awareness of *other* overrode awareness of self. *Other* filled all my thoughts and all my desires.

141

If only, I sighed and felt my own thoughts echoed from beyond. Or perhaps I was echoing that longing. Could it possibly be that *other* yearned for me as much as I yearned for it?

I say 'it' for truly I could not conceive of either male or female. Those thoughts evaded my mind at such distance that I would not find them for many ages. But the idea that two beings could be so drawn together by desire flooded me. If desire exists, surely satisfaction must also be possible. I floated on a new emotion as I found hope.

What I would do for *other*.

Of course, I had no means of doing. I was, for all intents and purposes, non-corporeal. Yet, I felt as I touched *other* with my mind, my awareness, that even this gave it some peace. I bathed in anger and madness when I awoke to my being, but as *other* tickled my consciousness into cognizance, I leapt from passion to sadness to despair to hope.

I felt the soft brush of flesh on my body. The very thought of having a physical existence with which to express my emotions filled me with joy. I wanted to test my limbs as I felt them take shape. I wanted to leap, to grasp, to run, to hold. What could I do with this body that suddenly encompassed my emotions.

Other skillfully, but with tenderness, bathed my body in light so pure that I wept for the sheer magnitude of my being.

I could feel! Not just the emotions I found inexplicably in my mind, but the gentle caress on my skin. I could feel the loving care with which my boundaries were explored. This is me. This is *other*. With touch came my first genuine contact with identity. My breath caught in unseen lungs as I was massaged and manipulated. Muscles took shape beneath my skin. Structure. A skeleton that gave rigidity to my stance. And with structure I found boldness. No matter how locked to my environment, I stood firm. I was one with my world and I embraced it as it touched me.

I absorbed all I could feel. I had known no other senses and now there was a mysterious world unfolding around me. I felt the hard stone where I was seated, its edge pressing into my thigh. I cherished the feeling. Where before there had been nothing, now sharpness began at a pinpoint and radiated outward, causing muscles to tense and flex as I sought comfort. The cloth, draped casually over my arm, was soft and warm, unlike the cold hardness of the stone. And across my shoulders, down my chest, there was a movement of air. Breath against my skin. *Other*.

My scalp tingled with delight as hair grew from my head. And suddenly, I knew by its absence what silence was. I had not known I lived in silence. But now, hearing the whistle of a bird, the rustle of cloth, gentle brushing, the sigh of breath... now I knew what silence had been. I had ears with which to hear.

The soft breath on my ear brought with it the sound of *other's* voice.

"I don't hate them. I did, but not any longer. I'm just through with them. They can't conceive that their actions hurt others. Or their inactions. A word could bring such all-consuming joy, yet it's absence is such pain and sorrow that I cannot help but weep. Would it be so difficult to say, 'I love you?' Does saying the words cause them pain? Or is love itself but latent pain?"

I love you. I savored the words in my mind. This. Love. This combining of all the emotions I had learned with the physical senses of my body must be love. Hate, Anger, Passion, Madness, Sorrow, Despair, Hope, Joy, Touch, Sound. All taken together, I knew love. *I love you.*

"Worse yet are those who say the words but can't abide by them. Those who swear to be with you always but then leave without a trace. Forsworn, forsaken, forgotten, and forlorn. And yet, he was so earnest. He loved me like no other, but he was just like all the rest. He left and went to war. A woman needs... *I* need more than that."

A woman. I knew, now, the voice of *other* was woman. I had no frame of reference for woman. Yet I defined her in my mind. Woman was the perfect complement to me. We would match. Woman would mold around me and fill those spaces within me where there was nothing, as I would fill her heart. She had voice. I had hearing. The voice was musical. It did not screech or scold like the distant bird. The voice was like her touch. She was firm and precise, but gentle and soft. Each touch, each word, sparked more passion. Whether she spoke of her anger, her disappointment, or her love, she was passionate. Her breath caressed and raised my ardor where it touched me, even when it cooled the temperature of my skin. She stroked along my body from my hair to my toes, each inch coming alive with her touch. This was woman. She gave life, gave being. She breathed sweetness into my soul and called forth the best that I could offer. *I will not forsake you.*

And her scent...

Scent? What new sensation was this that aroused and inflamed and flushed my skin?

I could smell the oil and turpentine. They were near. But they were a part of me and easily filtered out. One never noticed, I supposed, one's own odor. But wafting to my newly opened nostrils was a pale essence of almond and the heady scent of woman. There was a pungent aroma that accompanied her breath. Chamomile. The words identifying the scent accompanied it. I would learn to love this as well. It changed as days progressed.

Time now had meaning. It was measured in seconds we were together and hours we were apart.

I could feel my environment taking shape around me. Through the sound of her voice, I learned of life. I basked in the glow of her attention, even when she was not directly touching me. I was connected to everything around me through her. I could feel the coolness of the window, the warmth of the fire, the bitterness of the past, and the passion of the present.

"Love inflames me," she said. "I can't think when I am in love. I can only feel. I feel such a strong connection that I cannot separate myself from my lover. I don't ask myself if this is right or if this is good for me. I am so inflamed that I'm consumed by my lover. When he touches me, I am aroused. I don't *need* anything else. It is enough to know I am the source of his pleasure. That is pleasure to me. So why am I surprised that he turns from me and takes pleasure from someone else? I'm not enough. Eventually, he will leave me. Even the one who came to stay."

I felt the splash of moisture touch my cheek and wondered at the sense of loss I felt. I longed to reach out to her and caress her skin the way she touched mine. If only I could make her feel what she does to me, there would be no doubt left in her mind. But I am passive, unresisting as she works around me, unable to make the sounds that she makes.

Reach out to me. Touch me. I will love you always. Don't search for another. Don't hold yourself from me. I worship you. Free me from this silence that binds me. I love you. I will never forsake you.

"I know how foolish it is. I am not an automaton. I have needs. I know how to pleasure myself. I know at least one man who could give me that pleasure, as well." She hummed to herself as she arranged the bedding. It was soft, and while it would provide warmth when we were tucked beneath, it was cool to the touch. The crisply pressed sheets caressed my skin where they touched me. "Of course, he's gone. I'm sure he didn't mean to go. I know he loved me. I'm sure he intended to come back. But war... But war."

A sob and a clatter and she was gone.

Don't leave me. I am here for you. Please be here for me.

I wondered if I would ever be able to make sounds like she made. Would she hear? I would pour my heart out to her. I would bring her into my world; I would show her what love and devotion truly are. But an immense gulf separated us, even when we were together. Some undefinable difference between self and other that I could not cross. I could not break free of the scene that bound me. She could not see past her grief to where I waited.

I wondered how it was that I could feel so intensely what she felt, but could not communicate the depth of my love. She had added grief and loss to my repertoire of emotion. And I found that with each addition, my love grew.

Was I woman, too? Was I one of the hateful *he* who hurt her? I would not be. I would love her, care for her, protect her, hold her. I would be whatever she wanted... whatever she needed me to be. And I would wait here in this unfinished emptiness for her to find me and love me.

"Lush lips, my perfect man," she said. "Not lips drawn thin in anger or anemia. Not fattened by overindulgence and violence. Lush. Kissable. Soft to nibble around the edges of my areolae but muscular enough to latch onto my nipples. The pinch of lips on my sensitive nips. And if you are good at it, there are other sensitive bits you could nibble on." She almost sang as she worked.

And into the mix of my senses, I tasted mint on my tongue and felt the heat of lust in my groin. Water passed between my lips and I greedily sucked it down, wondering if this was the nipple she wanted me to touch. My sense of smell was magnified until it burst in my mouth, stung my lips, and forced my throat to open to its flavor. I could smell her and so sensitive were my newly awakened taste buds that I could savor the sweet and pungent moisture of her arousal. This nectar was all I wanted to live on. I would drink from her ever-flowing fount and use my tongue in combination with the lips of which she sang praises. A nibble, a lick. My face would glide through her moisture and I would bring her the pleasure of love.

"I am aroused today, my lovely man. It was the dream I had last night. It left me on edge, unable to come to completion.

You spoke to me. You spoke soft words of love in my ear—the dream so real, I could feel your breath. Do you dream of me in your little two-dimensional world? I think I'm finally losing it. I'm talking to a painting. But I don't think I will ever let you go. You are so easy to talk to. And you will never leave me for another. You will never march off to war. You will never grow cold and distant."

A painting? I knew I was a creation, but even now, I had no concept of why that would hold us apart. She was my goddess, giver of life. Surely, she was one with her creation. When I was complete—when I was whole—when she had made me into her perfect mate—I would hold her in these arms and taste her sweet lips with my own.

I love you. I am drawn to you with every breath. Feel my breath on your ear as I kiss you and take me in your arms as I love you. You are my whole being, my reason for existing. I love you.

My face tingled with the touch of her brush. *Let there be light! And there was light.* An explosion in my senses so intense that I lost touch with myself and floated in the brightness. And gradually I began to distinguish one color from another. I could see the color of her passion, her sorrow, her creativity, her love. My eyes had been opened to a new world.

"My ideal man, my love. I could make your eyes any color of the rainbow. They could be dark and brooding or limpid pools. They could be a witchery of gold and hazel or a warm and mossy green. I think—no I know, for I have always known you in my heart—that your eyes are the blue of the ocean's depths, reflecting the light of the sun and the image of your lover. I will ever be reflected in your eyes."

Shapes began to form as she continued her work. Around me were the things that I had sensed as sound, touch, taste, and smell. The bed, awaiting my lover and me, was turned down and covered with silky sheets. The pillow that cushioned me against the stone wall was soft and fluffy. The fire that burned on the hearth was warm and welcoming. I could hear it crackling and smell its smoke.

But before me stood the goddess. *Other*. Had I not known before, I would instantly have understood what her otherness was. We were different. My shoulders were broad, my stomach flat, my muscles hard beneath my almost translucent skin. She was soft and had no hard edges. Her long hair was pulled back in a knot. Her hips were broad and from her chest blossomed curves that I knew immediately were meant for my lips. Between her legs, where the scent of her womanhood rose, was a thick thatch of curly brown hair. Between my legs… there was nothing. Perhaps she would place her scent there, as well.

She was perfection. I was a poor image of her, chiseled and hardened into *he*.

"Ah, your eyes. There is a hunger there. You look at me as if to worship me and I see myself reflected there. I think I will never let another woman stand before you. I would be too jealous to see your hungry eyes cast upon her." She cleaned her brushes and set her palette aside. She stood boldly in front of me and I wanted to cast my eyes down because her glory was so great. "You like what you see. I'm not as trim as I was as a youth. Time has taken its toll. But my butt does not sag overly much," she said, turning her back to me and lifting her nether cheeks in her hands. I felt my heart pounding within my chest. She turned back. "Nor do my breasts. I'm a pretty well-preserved old bat. That's only by comparison to you. You are but days old. I am ancient by comparison. Why have I never met you? You, my wonderful ideal man. Goodnight, my darling."

She turned and left me to my thoughts, my head filled with the vision of her beauty. And a greater yearning awoke in me than I had known before. Her image was burned into my retina and wherever I looked I saw her.

Come to me. I will take care of you. Teach me how to please you and I will ever be your mate. I love you. I love you.

Now that I had eyes, I could see where I stood. Things looked different than they felt. My world had been limited to my canvas, but now I gazed out upon a different reality. My little cozy fire was a mere reflection of the fire that burned in the hearth and it stayed lit when that other fire had gone to ash. Beyond my easel, her chair sat. Brushes, pots of paint, and other paintings all were within my vision. I wondered if I, too, would end up propped against a wall as she went on to create something more wonderful. I sensed no consciousness from the other subjects. Surely if they longed as I did, I would have felt it.

And, though I had a sense of time passing before, now I saw day turn to night and day again. And again. As I waited.

Come to me. I will love you. I will be your lover.

"Why?" she asked as she came into the room. She shed the smock she wore as she came into the studio. This was her norm—to be naked as she worked. She picked up her brushes and palette and began mixing my skin tones, darkening them slightly. "Why do you fill my dreams? Why has the only climax I have known in weeks been when I dreamed of you? And even now, I blush knowing that you are looking at my nakedness. I know your desire."

I felt a stirring in my groin. My maleness took shape. Her touch caused my heart to skip and I hardened beneath her caress.

"Fine. Firm. Not grotesquely huge. A perfect fit. You lean back so casually with your erection proudly displayed for me to see. And I know it is me you are looking at that makes your manhood so proud. Look at me. I am wet from imagining you pressing toward me. Into me." Her brushes clattered to the floor and she leaned back in her chair, her legs spread before me. Her fingers moved rapidly, flicking the small protrusion between her nether lips. My priapic core strained against my pelvis searching for that perfect union I knew awaited me between her legs. And as she gasped her climax, my heart stopped as I suffered death and life anew.

"There is only one thing to do," she sobbed as her own little death released her. "I cannot leave you in that condition and I would not have you gelded. You must have a mate."

A mate! You are my mate! I love you. I pray to you, my goddess; join me here. Let me fill you, fulfill you. Let me embrace you in my arms.

With her next strokes, a warm softness pressed against me. My hand caressed flesh for the first time.

It was so different than the other things I sensed. Not hard like the stone, nor cold like the silk sheets. Not hot like the fire, but every bit as consuming. I held out my arms and she filled them with her body. Our foreplay filled in the details of her body. I could touch her! Her leg wrapped around my thigh. Her breasts pressed against my chest and I felt the tiny nubs that she said were her nipples. Her hair fell across my arm. Her breath touched my cheeks. Her lips touched my lips and I strained forward once again to reach her swollen sex.

Sex. Yes, an awakened desire to be fully immersed in her body.

I love you.

"Then love me."

Had she spoken an answer to my plea? Had she, at long last, heard my words and responded? Her lips were on my lips and her mouth opened to my probing. Her taste had the lingering bitterness of coffee and chocolate. I savored her tongue. I caressed her breasts and felt their fullness in my hand. The round plumpness of her bottom filled my other hand. She grabbed my hair and held my mouth to hers, both of us gasping for breath.

I felt the soft, hot moisture at our middle open to let me enter.

Every nerve ending in my body fired and came alive. As I moved in her, I felt our bodies become one. I felt the soft tickle of her pubic hair against my groin and the dampness mat our hair in tangles with each other. Her warm breath on my cheek and the moisture of her tears on my face. The scent of her arousal increased my own. I was driven to new depths in her body, finding that place where I could fill her emptiness as she drove the darkness from my soul.

Now I knew. I knew I was alive.

And this time—this time when the muscles now surrounding my manhood began to pulse and vibrate with her impending climax, my orgasm responded. The tightness between my legs erupted and I felt the contractions begin at the base of my spine and rocket through my entire body. I flooded her. The soul she had given me, I poured out within her.

She cried out, clutching me to her. I felt her spasms grasping me. I held her as her bones threatened to dissolve in the passion of our union.

"What have I done?" she cried out. Her eyes opened wide and I saw my own reflected in them. "What have you done?"

"My darling, my goddess, I have loved you," I said. My voice! A reality that I never thought to hear. My love resting her head against my chest. "I have called and you have answered. And you have loved me."

We turned our heads slightly and looked back to that other reality. That world she had forsaken to join me in mine. The artist's brush lay on the floor beside the hardening palette. She turned in my arms, her lips touching mine again, her eyes seeking assurance.

"I love you. I will never forsake you," I whispered.

Her colors blended with my own. And we were caught forever in each other's eyes.

This story was inspired by a reviewer of my work. "'If a picture paints a thousand words…', a phrase from a 70s hit from Bread; Devon turns that on its head, and uses thousands of words to paint a picture. Almost lyrical at times, this long story grips the reader, and holds him/her until the end."

I love art. I love drawing, singing, sculpting. But I'm not very good at it. My medium is words. And so, I wrote this story to discover whether the ideal lover could be painted with a thousand words. The unlikely artist is an advertising copywriter. If he can describe toothpaste, razor blades, and deodorant well enough to attract buyers, why not attract his perfect mate… with a thousand words?

A THOUSAND WORDS

THE PENCIL lead broke. He was pressing too hard again. The more he tried, the harder it became until his frustration caused him to tense up and ruin another drawing. Why couldn't he have real talent? Why couldn't he make his hand draw what his mind could see so clearly? He felt like a person he'd seen auditioning for a talent show. She believed in herself but didn't have any talent. Everyone cringed at her offkey rendition. She put her heart into it, but just wasn't any good.

The difference was that the talentless rock star wannabe didn't know she couldn't sing. She thought she was the next great thing that would take the world by storm. Ian *knew* he didn't have the talent it took to be a great artist. It wasn't that he was less passionate about it or that he couldn't draw at all. He'd taken classes. He'd filled sketchbooks. He could do a decent rendering from a photograph in pencil. He really couldn't paint that well. And give him a live model and his sketches barely came out looking human.

He wanted to be an artist, but all he had was broken pencils.

"GREAT JOB ON this campaign, Ian," Jack said as they left the meeting room. "I don't know how you come up with these ideas, but recasting the commercial for men's deodorant from the perspective of a woman was brilliant. You can really think like a woman. It's not new to use a woman to make the man want to please her, but to actually market to the woman to get her to buy it for her man is a breakthrough. Nice job."

"Thanks, Jack. It's just trying to look at everything from a new angle."

"You're the most creative guy we have on the staff. Next time, though, get Georgia to help you on the artwork for the proposal. It was the only weak spot. You know what they say—a picture's worth a thousand words."

"Will do."

Ian went into his office seething. Most creative guy on staff and he couldn't draw. He knew the storyboard looked cartoon-ish, but it was the best he could do. Georgia wasn't likely to be much help. She only wanted to draw her own ideas, not some-one else's.

A picture might be worth a thousand words, but when all you had was words, that's what you had to use. It worked, but this client was ready for a big change in its approach. He could turn the whole thing over to Georgia or Burk to develop the collaterals. Then it would be a miracle if they turned out the way he'd described them. Georgia's standard mantra was "I can make it so much better than that."

He swiveled in his chair and stared out the twenty-first-floor window at the lake. The office faced east and none of the 'artists' wanted it because the light was bad. At least he didn't have to worry about that when he was writing. He'd researched and purchased ceramic window film and installed it himself. He couldn't tell the difference between natural light and the filtered light. He could see out his windows just fine and there was no glare from the morning sun on his computer screen.

The artists, of course, hated it. They wouldn't show their work in his office. They had to have the conference room with north facing windows and 5000K lighting. He wondered exactly how many of their clients or their clients' customers would look at the artwork under those precise conditions.

He often sneaked the artwork into his office to see if he could tell a difference. He couldn't.

AT HOME ALONE, Ian ate heated-up leftovers from the night before. The food was good, even coming out of the microwave. It wasn't that he couldn't cook. But he didn't really know how to cook for *one*. Everything he made was the way his Northside mother had made it—in quantity. He cooked once or twice a week and ate the leftovers the other nights. Sundays were reserved for steak, grilled on the balcony of his apartment.

He wondered if he could learn to cook for two, should the occasion ever arise. Not that it was likely to. He'd had 'relationships' before. But they always seemed to end up the same. They both left disappointed that it wasn't what they expected or hoped for. It wasn't heartrending. It wasn't filled with screaming and hatred. It was just a creeping sadness that came over them before they said goodbye.

He could see *her* in his mind's eye. He spent hours trying to draw her, to no avail. There was always something missing. The pictures in his mind simply weren't complete. Still, he knew she was out there. Somewhere.

"WHY DON'T YOU ever ask me out?" Georgia demanded as she threw the drawings down on his desk. They were working on a new campaign for shampoo. It appeared they had become the go-to team for personal care products. "I always make your ideas so much better."

She'd changed his concept in the renderings again. He'd had a simple image in mind of a guy out running and playing with his dog. Big, hairy dog. He wasn't sure what kind. After a long day, he comes home hot and sweaty and takes a shower. The shampoo bottle was in the picture with the brand name clearly recognizable. Then the camera pans down to the dog—same color hair—with lather all over him. Cut to the guy opening his door to a beautiful woman. Next, there are a woman's hands running through his luxurious hair. Pull back, see the woman petting the dog and the tag, "Be careful where you use it."

Her concept might have been considered sexier because the woman was in the shower with the man and dog and as he shampoos her hair, she does the dog. It just missed all the humor and the poignancy of the original.

"No, you don't," he sighed. "You make the idea yours, but not better. In fact, you lose half the concept when you try to make it better. You're a fucking illustrator, not a concept person. Just draw what I ask for and quit trying to make it better."

He admitted, he was angry. This wasn't the campaign he wanted to put words around. The images were sexy, but the point was lost. He wondered if Burk could do any better, but he'd used up his company resource allotment. If he wanted something different, he'd have to pay for it himself. That was the way Georgia worked. She used up his resources and he never had anything to spend on something better.

That, he decided, was the problem with women.

IN A THOUSAND words or less, Ian could describe exactly what he wanted in an ad, could create the emotional impact, and could sell an entire campaign. Why couldn't he draw the pictures himself? Sometimes he swore stick figures would be more effective than trying to rewrite an entire campaign to meet the illustration that his art team came up with.

"Great presentation, Ian," Jack said. Jack was the account manager and the product du jour was toothpaste. Ian just couldn't wait until they were doing suppositories. *What a fucking job.* "Where was Georgia today? She did good work on this one."

"It wasn't Georgia's art," Ian grumbled. "I can't work with her."

"What? We can't afford to go outside the company for concept art! Ian, you have to use the resources we have."

"I paid for it out of my pocket. Jack, every time Georgia gets hold of my concepts I end up having to rewrite everything to match her art. She had the guy squeezing hair gel onto his toothbrush instead of the toothpaste. I'm through with her."

"You can't dump her, Ian."

"Yes, I can. I know you're sleeping with her, Jack. God! The whole office knows. She had the gall to ask me when *I* was going to take her out. Hope you know that she'll sleep with anyone here to be the star, including you. I won't use her again," Ian said. Jack scowled at him.

"She's more valuable than you are, Ian. She can draw. Get over it," Jack growled.

"Let's see what she can come up with on her own, then. Just give her your next project and quit using me as an intermediary."

"IAN, THIS IS a pretty heavy accusation," Floyd said. Ian sat across the desk from the CEO of the advertising firm. "We've always been pleased with your work, but the complaint from Jack about you being unable to work as a team with your fellow employees seems to be supported. We're going to have to put you on probation. Work with your resources or pack your desk."

Ian sat staring at the old-school exec. He still wore a three-piece suit, had three-martini lunches, and was fucking at least three of the women in the company. Ian could see the film clip in his mind. "A Triple Threat." He started to chuckle.

"I don't see the humor in your situation," Floyd said.

"Mr. Anderson, find another writer. Oh, and I'd suggest you have the illustrations finished before you ask him to do a campaign so all he has to do is caption them." Ian walked out of the CEO's office and grabbed a banker's box from the storeroom. It was too big for the personal possessions he had in his office.

For a moment, he was tempted to strip the ceramic film off the windows, but that was petty and he wouldn't be able to use it elsewhere anyway. He did stop long enough to run a format program on his hard drive and wipe all his personal files. He stopped at the receptionist's desk and gave her an inventory of the items in his box and had her check off each item. Then he walked out the door. Unemployed.

IAN NEEDED HIS income. He had three months' cash in reserve. All his other savings were tied up in long term IRAs for his comfortable retirement. He might have to live on dogfood until then. It was a long time away. Monday, he would have to hit the street looking for a new position.

He needed to find an agency where content was more important than presentation. If he could find an agency where the content and presentation were equally important, it was possible that he could manage a good working relationship. Collaboration. That's what it was all about. An image was nothing without the words that went with it.

Take that painting at the Met he liked so much. Simply describing the painting wasn't enough. A girl... woman? Definitely female... in a dress stood on a balcony looking out over a cityscape. In the distance light reflected off the lake behind which mountains arose. One hand was placed casually on the rail. It's an old-fashioned balustrade, so the scene could be any time from the Renaissance to the present. Balconies, lakes, cities, and mountains coincided in dozens of countries all over the world. There was not enough detail in the city or the dress to identify a period or location. It was a great advertising illustration. He could write an ad for soap, champagne, perfume, designer clothing, or tourism off that illustration. The key would be how it was worded. He could write a tragedy or a romance or a comedy based on that image alone.

*It had been a long day, but the evening approached, rife
with anticipation. She could smell the excitement in the
air. Her true love was out there somewhere – gallant
and handsome and invisible. He did not even know she
existed. A cool breeze blew her hair across her face and
its tickle against her ears caused the bumps to rise on
her flesh – including those touchstones of her arousal
pressing against the fabric of her dress. Her eyes drifted
closed. So many possibilities. With her hand on the balustrade she flexed her knees and leapt to the cold embrace
of the courtyard below.*

Perhaps that message would have been more to the point
than Shakespeare's rendering of the same scene. They end up
the same.

*It had been a long day, but the evening had been
enchanted. She could smell the excitement in the air.
True love. Was it ever possible? He was gallant and
handsome and she loved him to the bottom of her soul.
But he didn't even know she existed. A cool breeze blew
her hair across her face and its tickle against her ears
caused the bumps to rise on her flesh – including those
touchstones of her arousal pressing against the fabric
of her dress. Her eyes drifted closed. So many possibilities. She sighed, "Romeo. Romeo. Wherefore art thou
Romeo?"*

Or perhaps there was a less doomed version of the same
scene. Something in which the lovers find each other. Perhaps
the same scene made her smile or laugh.

*It had been a long day, but the evening approached
with the expectation of celebration. She could smell the
excitement in the air. Her gallant and handsome true
love was near and she loved him to the bottom of her
soul. A cool breeze blew her hair across her face and
its tickle against her ears caused the bumps to rise on*

*her flesh – including those touchstones of her arousal
pressing against the fabric of her dress. Her eyes drifted
closed. So many possibilities. The strains of the minstrels
below wafted up to her aerie and she smiled at their
antics. "Are you ready, my love?" he asked coming up
behind her. "So ready," she responded, welcoming his
embrace and the hot touch of his lips to hers.*

What his agency hadn't understood was that it was his words that sold the message. The artwork supported it. Somewhere, there must be an agency that understood.

Just like somewhere there must be a woman who was right for him. He sighed, his own picture of winsome frustration as he stood on the tiny balcony of his apartment. Maybe that was why he couldn't draw. He was too caught up in the words and the picture they painted in his mind to put a feeble stroke of a brush on the paper.

Or maybe he just didn't have any talent.

HE'D BEEN HITTING the pavement for four weeks. Figuratively. No one literally went door-to-door to hunt for a job these days. He sat in front of his computer for hours each day searching job sites and taking online courses on getting an interview, effective interviewing, and goal setting. His bottle of Laphroaig was almost empty. Second bottle. Who cares? It was the weekend and he could have a drink in the afternoon if he wanted. It just didn't seem to do anything. He took another sip and then tossed the rest into the back of his mouth.

If he was going to drink it like that, he could buy cheaper scotch. He returned to his computer to work through yet another self-improvement course.

*Set SMART (specific, measurable, attainable, relevant
and time-bound) goals that motivate you and write them
down to make them feel tangible. Then plan the steps*

*you must take to realize your goal, and cross off each one
as you work through them.*

*The first step in setting personal goals is to consider
what you want to achieve in your lifetime (or at least, by
a significant and distant age in the future). Setting lifetime goals gives you the overall perspective that shapes
all other aspects of your decision making.*

Well, that was the first problem. What did he want? A job.
A life. A woman. He laughed out loud when he filled out the
form. The way he felt right now, the right woman could make
about any job or life tolerable. None of those desires, though,
were very specific. He could accept any job, but he couldn't
accept just any woman. He thought about Georgia at the office
and shuddered. What did he really want in a woman? Besides
his cock.

Ian took a drawing pad and a pencil to the balcony and sat
on his lounger. Hmm. If he was going to have a woman in his
life, he should get another chair. Or maybe he should trade this
one in on a double. The woman he wanted in his life wasn't one
who sat on the other side of the balcony.

Who was she? He closed his eyes and tried to imagine her.
He should be job hunting. He wasn't going to attract a young
woman by sitting on the balcony daydreaming. Hmm. That
was one criterion. He jotted it down.

She's a young woman. Well, that was a bit egotistical. Why
would a young woman want a forty-some-year-old failure?
Young women wanted money. If she was a *beautiful* young
woman, she wanted a lot of money. And besides, who wanted
to put up with a person who was just starting out in life and
had to discover all the things that he'd already been through.
It wasn't really *young* that he wanted. It was more… *youthful.*

*She's youthful in appearance and action, though prob-
ably older than she looks. She stays healthy and fit
because she has an active life, not because she obsesses*

over it. She's not just youthful; she makes me feel younger when I'm with her. She encourages me to be healthy and fit by being a person I want to keep up with.

He looked at his drawing pad. He'd always avoided writing on drawing paper because he was supposed to draw on drawing paper. That's why it was called *drawing* paper. He had flimsy sheets of yellow legal pads for writing. That was *writing* paper. But somehow, looking at those words on the substantial drawing paper, it seemed right. He was going to paint a picture on the page. Only he was going to use a thousand words.

IAN WAS CALLED for an interview on Monday and gladly sat with the director and an account manager for nearly two hours as they grilled him about his work and portfolio. Portfolios are different today than they were back when. When he'd taken his college portfolio to his first job interview, it was a thick binder filled with stories, ad copy, sketches, and two video tapes. Now he carried a laptop, showed a presentation, and ran some YouTube videos.

"Why did you leave Anderson? It looked like you had a lot going for you, including over ten years with the firm," Mr. Melrose said. I had to laugh.

"This is a business where you stick your neck out on a regular basis and risk getting your head chopped off," Ian said. "That means you have to have enough ego invested in the project to believe it is the best the client can get. I've got a good record of successful campaigns, but the best were ideas that I presented before creative got hold of them. I was told that I had to use the resources available, but they felt it was their right to make changes without looping me in to discuss them. I was continually coming up to a presentation and discovering that the visuals didn't match what I'd written at all. I had to adjust on the fly, sometimes getting surprised during a client meeting by my account manager and artist. Most of the time, they were good ideas. They just weren't as good as the ones I'd put together. I'm no artist, but the campaigns I showed you — and I know you were already familiar with them — were the best. Those were the campaigns that I presented to the client with my own pretty meager art skills for the renderings. I was told that showing my art made the company look bad and I had to use our creative group. I simply couldn't get the results I needed. So, I left. Ego. I've got my share of it, Mr. Melrose, but I don't let that get in the way of putting the best product out there."

"I think we'd need to have you meet with our creative group to see if you could establish a working relationship with them," Melrose said. "I don't mind telling you that I have a lot of faith in our creative department. Maybe we can do a test project as a consultant."

The interview ended without a commitment. Ian wasn't going to compromise his values or creative control on a project, even if it meant he needed to eat Ramen noodles for the next month.

WITH THE LAST of his scotch and his sketchbook, Ian sat on his balcony looking at the lights of the city and began to dream about what he'd like to do in life with the woman of his dreams.

She wants to travel and see the country – the world.
She's a free spirit and is ready to go at the drop of a
hat. She packs light so we can fly to Paris or hitchhike
to Disneyland. She's up for the cheap way to get there
because the journey is as exciting as the destination. If
there is an adventure to be had, she is ready to take it.
If we can't find an adventure, we'll make one up. She's
not a daredevil or adrenalin junkie – if she jumps out
of an airplane it's because the plane is crashing. But
flying along behind a boat on a kite? She'd find that fun.

She's not concerned about money. Between us, we have enough to live simply and fulfill dreams. She doesn't accumulate stuff. She knows she might need to leave it all behind to do something new.

IAN WASN'T CALLED in for another interview, nor was he given a project as a consultant. He didn't go online for three days. Instead, he focused on the pad of drawing paper with a No.2 pencil and his dream of the perfect woman for him. And before his eyes, she took shape in 1,000 words.

She's youthful in appearance and action, though she is probably older than she looks. She stays healthy and fit because she has an active life. It's not just that she's youthful; she makes me feel younger when I'm with her. She encourages me to be healthy and fit by being a person I want to keep up with.

She's pretty. That doesn't mean she's a fashion model or a Playboy centerfold. She has a pretty face and smile. She lights up a room when she smiles and I respond by thinking, "Gee, she's pretty!" When she turns that smile toward me, I feel like the most important person in the universe. My smile, in turn, tells her she is the most beautiful woman in the world. The rest of her body complements that smile. It reflects the beauty I see when I look in her eyes. She turns me on. I desire her.

A picture can only show how she looks, but what's inside is even more important. She's smart. She doesn't need to be a Rhodes Scholar to prove it, though that would be okay. She has a broad life view with experience to back it up. She sees past petty issues that crop up and stays focused on the big things. She reads and investigates to find out what is true and what isn't.

She has ideas. Lots of ideas. And she likes to talk about them. We have long discussions about things that no one else would think of. Her voice is clear and even when she speaks quietly, I have no problem hearing her. It's like she's attuned to my ears. When we've talked about an idea – maybe an article we read, a book, a movie, or deep philosophical musings – she embraces the silence. We can sit enjoying each other's company for hours without saying anything.

She's funny – sometimes by accident and sometimes by design. She has a good sense of humor and can see the lighter side of almost any situation. She likes to laugh. She thinks I'm funny, too, though not necessarily funny-looking. She smiles at me and makes a face when I say something stupid, then breaks out laughing.

She wants to travel and see the country – the world. She's a free spirit and is ready to go at the drop of a hat. She packs light so we can fly to Paris or hitchhike to Disneyland. She's up for the cheap way to get there because the journey is as exciting as the destination. If there is an adventure to be had, she is ready to take it. If we can't find an adventure, we'll make one up. She's not a daredevil or adrenalin junkie – if she jumps out of an airplane it's because the plane is crashing. But flying along behind a boat on a kite – she'd find that fun. She's not concerned about money. Between us, we have enough to live simply and fulfill dreams. She doesn't accumulate a lot of stuff because she knows she might need to leave it all behind so we can do something new.

She doesn't need me. She wants me. She is complete, whole, and content with who she is, but likes being with me. She likes having me to plan with and to play with.

It's more fun, and she likes having fun. She has ideas about where to go and who to visit along the way, but doesn't need to be in any one place to be happy. She's happy when she is with me, and I am happy with her.

I'm not her last hope. She's not desperate for love, for a family, for sex, or for money. She's happy if any of those come her way as a bonus for being with me. She gives me a reason to get up in the morning, to work, to play, to adventure. And she gives me a reason to turn off my computer and go to bed at night. Both the getting up and the going to bed reasons fill my heart with joy.

She's comfortable in her own skin and makes me comfortable in it as well. If we're just hanging around, clothing is optional and usually discarded. She loves to cuddle and kiss. Feeling her skin against my skin sends a thrill through our bodies. We're happy to just be in touch, but if something else comes up, we're happy for that, too.

Her spiritual side is revealed in the way she cares about other people, the land, the animals. She might have a religion, but she doesn't feel compelled to convert anyone to it, nor does she have patience for people trying to convert her. It is deeply personal and respected by both of us. Our shared spiritual experience is in the sunset, the waves lapping on the shore, the stark desert, the lush jungle, and the depth of our love. In these things, we come together as one heart and soul.

She appreciates my unique talent and has a talent that I can equally appreciate. Recognizing each other's strengths, we can collaborate on new and creative projects that bring us both fulfillment and joy.

We share simple needs, have simple desires, eat simple food, drink simple wine. We don't overindulge because when we are with each other, we have plenty of stimulation we can enjoy with clear heads. She keeps her wits

*about her, even if I'm near to losing mine. She's neat
and tidy, but doesn't get stressed out if I leave the dishes
until morning.*

*Most of all, she wants to be with me for this part
of our journey and if we grow apart as companions or
lovers, we will still be together as friends. Our relationship is built on respect, trust, and care for each other.
From that comes love.*

IAN READ WHAT he'd written. He'd spent hours erasing and
rewriting. He looked again at the rules for setting goals. Specific.
Measurable. Attainable. Relevant. Time-bound. He added a line.

She is out there and I will find her within a year.

He looked at the empty scotch bottle that hadn't been
touched in three days and tossed it in the recycling. He ran hot
water in the kitchen sink and washed the dishes, dried them,
and put them away. He pulled out his little vacuum cleaner
and ran it across the floors before taking all the accumulated
garbage and recycling to their repositories. He stripped his bed,
gathered his dirty clothes, and went to the laundry room. He
sat watching the clothes tumble in the dryer and thought about
what he wanted.

What is it that she wants from me?

"IAN, IT'S FLOYD Anderson," the voice said when Ian
answered his phone.

"Hello, Mr. Anderson. Did I fail to complete the exit interview?" Ian asked. He couldn't imagine why his former boss
would be calling.

"Let's leave it at Floyd. We've been too formal for too long,"
Anderson said. "How's your vacation? Ready to get back to
work?"

"It's been productive," Ian hedged. He'd cleaned his apartment and written a description of his ideal woman. That was productive.

"Melrose isn't going to call you, Ian. We talked."

"You blackballed me?"

"Quite the opposite. I gave you a very good recommendation. I was glad you were considering a good agency," Anderson said. "They went behind you. They hired Jack and Georgia."

"Shit."

"No loss here. They hadn't sold a campaign since you left. I found out a lot of things that hadn't surfaced before you left. None of them were good." Anderson cleared his throat and began his pitch. Ian could recognize the change in tenor. He was going to be sold something. He waited.

"This is a cut-throat business as you well know, Ian. We have good employee retention here because we've tried to compensate our people fairly and provide a positive work environment. Sometimes we mess up on that and lose an employee who was truly valuable, like you, Ian. It usually plays out on the other side. Employees use us as a stepping stone into a better, more lucrative, or more powerful position. That's what happened with Jack and Georgia. They'd been planning their move for over a year and Melrose had just hired them when he interviewed you. Jack is now the Vice President of Sales and he took Georgia and Stew with him. When he found out you had interviewed, he said he wouldn't have you on his team. That's why you won't be hired."

"It's a blessing. If I'd gone there and found he was the boss, I'd have quit on the spot. A short-lived employment record."

"That's the thing, Ian. You weren't using us as a stepping stone. You liked your job here and you were good at it. You left out of principle. Few people in this industry have those. It took me a while to figure that one out, but when I discovered how long it had taken for you to get an interview at Melrose, I realized you didn't have a plan for leaving our agency. That's why I want you to come back," Anderson said. "I need a man with principles to run creative and sell our big ideas."

"Run creative?"

"That's right. I know your strength is writing. You'll do a lot of it. But I want to infuse our whole new team with the kind of principles you demonstrated. We've got the opportunity to bid the entire marketing campaign for Restore Youth. It's right up your alley and I'll give you full license to run the show. Come back, Ian. You'll like your new employment package and we have some crackerjack people lined up for you to interview to fill out your team. I've talked to those from the old team that are still here and they are enthused to have you take the reins. We need you, Ian. And I think you need us."

IAN COULDN'T BELIEVE he was walking back into his old office again. It was more accurate to say into his former employer's office. The office he was led to was formerly Jack's. It was a nice corner that overlooked the lake on one side and the city on the other. It was large enough to have a conference table as well as his desk and a small conversation grouping of comfortable chairs. If he needed to, he could live here. The office had a bar, microwave, refrigerator, and private bathroom. He didn't need to put filtering shades on the windows.

He tossed his briefcase on the table and looked around as the door clicked shut behind him. That had to change first off. He raised the shade on the sidelight and locked it so the window was fully exposed. The door opened inward to the other side and he pulled it all the way back against the wall. Lacking a doorstop, it would swing closed if he let go. He grabbed one of the comfy chairs and pushed it against the door to hold it open. Then he got out a yellow legal pad from his briefcase and wrote 'doorstop' at the top of the page. He'd make a shopping list or ask the supply room what they had.

The desk faced the door and his back would be to the window. The glare of morning light would hit his screen. He needed to rotate the desk so it was against the wall with the door to his right and the windows left and forward. He was just getting ready to shift the furniture when there was a knock at the door. Ian turned.

"Mr. Marx, I'm Davey from tech support. I'm here to get you set up on your computer, sir."

"Davey, I'm Ian," he answered. "I wonder if you could help me shift my desk before you set up my computer. I'd like it to face that way."

"Really? You don't want the power position?" Davey asked. "Mr. Delaney wanted people to see him as soon as they opened the door, like he was a god."

"People won't have to open the door to see me. If I'm in the office, I'll be visible when they walk by."

"I heard from a couple of the creative people who still work here that you were a little odd. That wasn't meant as an insult. Sorry!"

"No offense taken. Do I need to be here while you set up the computer?"

"Not until it's time to log on. I'll give you a temporary user ID and password. Change it as soon as you get back to the office. I'll write it down for you," Davey said when they finished moving the desk. It was heavy.

"I think I'll take a little walk through the department and talk to people as they come in."

Ian left his office and walked through the open workspace. When it was originally designed, it was intended to be a collaborative environment where artists chose a workstation to complement the work they had to do at that moment. No one had a permanent desk. There were drafting tables, easels, computer stations, and work areas where three or four people could turn to face each other and consult on a project. In theory, it was good. In fact, people still staked out their turf, claimed a workstation as their own, and were angry when someone else touched it. When Jack moved into the large corner office and closed the door, it solidified isolation as the desired workspace. He needed to resolve the issue with the older employees before he brought in new ones.

"Good morning, Lee," Ian said as the somewhat scatter-brained photographer came into the room.

"Ian! You're back! They said you would be, but I don't believe anything until I see it—and take a picture." He swung his camera up and snapped off a shot of Ian with a bemused expression on his face. "Great! That's just great!" Lee said.

"Can you set up to catch a candid of everyone this morning?" Ian asked. "I think we should have a gallery of photos on the wall over there. Feel free to add to it at any time, but try to keep it balanced and don't just take pictures of your favorite girl. Can you do that?"

"That'll be fun. I need to leave at nine to do a photoshoot for the 'Little Darlings' swimwear line. If I don't get everyone this morning, I'll just keep shooting until I have them all."

"We'll have some new people starting soon, too, so that shouldn't be a problem. Who did the concept?"

"Drake got with the new girl, Penny. They hashed out the whole thing as a joint project. It's sweet."

"That's good to hear. Do you have everything you need here in the office? How's your workspace?" Ian asked.

"I don't spend all that much time up here. We've got the studio on the 19th floor. I could use a bigger monitor for photo editing and better light control, but I think all the artists feel the same way," Lee said.

"That's good to know. I'll talk to everyone else, too." Ian made a note on his legal pad regarding the photo wall and the new monitors and lighting. For the rest of the morning, Ian talked to the staff as they got to work. Everyone echoed Lee's opinion about monitors and light. A few said the space was too noisy. Two people said they just wanted a single place they could go to and call their own.

"KNOCK-KNOCK. HI, IAN. I'm Penny," the bright redhead announced at his door. "Are you going to leave the door open all the time? It's great to be able to see out the window from the pit."

"Any time you need a light break, feel free to come in and stare out the window." *Wow! She was awesome.* Thirty-one, he knew from her HR file. He hadn't expected her bubbly personality or quirky beauty. It made him smile.

"Really? That would be great," she said. "I wasn't here this morning when you were talking to everyone because I was downstairs getting ready for the photo shoot. So, what do you want to know?" she asked. She plopped down on the sofa and put her feet on the coffee table. Ian leaned back in his chair and copied her move by putting his feet on his desk.

"How are you settling in?" he asked. "You've been here about six weeks now, right?"

"Yeah. Apparently, I got hired right after you left on vacation."

"I quit. I didn't go on vacation."

"Really? Everybody but that bitch artist, Georgia, said you'd be back soon. Jack said something about it being after he was dead and buried, but I guess he is." She was irreverent and flippant. Ian smiled. He was liking her.

"What about your workspace? How does our so-called open pit work for you?" He didn't expect her loud laugh.

"Open pit? Like the barbecue sauce?" Ian got the inadvertent joke.

"Well, I *am* grilling you."

"Believe me, when I'm on a project, you could stick me in the knee-hole under your desk and it wouldn't bother me. I can work anywhere." Ian put his feet down and looked under the desk. "Oh, God! I probably shouldn't have given you that image. I mean, I'm not really into... you know. That's why I have writers. I'm not safe writing my own material."

"How did the shoot go this morning?" Ian asked, ignoring the implication of her getting under his desk—or at least, trying to.

"It was a blast. Lee is a riot when he gets on-set. And Drake is a dream to work with. I think Little Darlings will love the promo. It starts with one of their little bikinis on a five-year-old. Then we have this totally stacked babe wearing it at the beach. The tagline is 'the swimwear you never grow out of.' We had a blast shooting the stills. You'd really think the little girl was the same person as the college girl."

"And it was your idea?"

"Oh, God, no! I just did the storyboard to interpret what Drake had written in his description. Then I worked with Lee to get the models in the right positions to work with the background art he'd found."

"So, we did the pictures of both models against a blue screen and cut them into a background? Sounds like some good planning."

"Lee was able to find stock beach scenes that we could use that were almost a perfect match for what I drew. It's really great working with him."

"Well, I'll let you get back to it. Thanks for stopping in when you were finished."

"No probs. If I get to be too much a nuisance sitting in your office staring out the window, though, kick me out!" She waved as she left and Ian sighed. He almost asked her out, but he was determined not to be *that* kind of boss. Still, if he met her outside the work environment, she'd be a perfect match for three items on his list. Maybe a lot more. He guessed he'd find out what she was really like to work with when they started the new Restore Youth campaign.

IAN WAS INTENSELY busy his first week on the job. Anderson already had vetted resumes of a dozen candidates that were scheduled for interviews. In the wake of Jack and Georgia leaving, several others had decided it was time for a change rather than stay to get dismissed. He had writers, designers, graphic artists, photographers, and videographers to interview.

In the midst of that, he began making subtle changes in the work environment. He kept the open design, but let the staff choose permanent workstations. Some resources were left as common to the group, but computers, cameras, and art supplies were considered part of a person's personal space. Lee's photos hit the wall on Friday morning and people started exclaiming about the new look of the office.

Ian also had to assemble the team he wanted to work with for Restore Youth. He met with the account manager and they spent an afternoon going over the RFP and the company's previous campaigns. The immediate focus would be on a new line of facial cremes, body lotion, and anti-wrinkle treatments. But if all went well, the company was interested in a complete rebranding that would stretch across all their products, including a chain of health resorts, fitness products, massage oils, and adult toys.

"OKAY, PEOPLE, THIS is the kickoff for the Restore Youth project," Ian said. "I've looked through everyone's portfolio, talked to each of you individually, and discussed the team requirements with Rick, our account manager. I expect this will be a project that keeps us busy for months if all goes well. Since some of you are new to the company, let's start with a round of introductions. I'm Ian Marx. This is our account manager Rick Davis. And you?" He pointed at Penny.

"Penny Liston, artist and all-round creative genius," she laughed.

"And on this project, Penny will take on the role of art director," Ian said. Penny looked up in surprise. Ian nodded at the next person at the table.

"Jill Soderman, graphic artist."

"Lee Williams, photographer."

"Drake Mallard, and stop laughing. I'm designated as associate writer."

"John Smith, and you can all laugh at that, too. It's my real name. I work in collateral."

And so the intros went. In addition to being the creative director, Ian would also function as the chief writer to launch the project, but hoped to hand off the bulk of the writing to Drake as the project progressed and they got in sync. They ordered in pizza for lunch as Rick gave the client briefing and they started brainstorming.

"It seems backwards to me," Penny said. "I don't think we'll succeed with the product and then the brand."

"Tell me what you're thinking," Ian said.

"We've got lots of examples in the industry of companies that were one product and built a brand around that product but were unable to move into an expanded product line without completely rebranding. I think we need a concept for the entire brand and then build the product campaign within it."

"But the company only wants the product campaign right now. They won't decide on a brand management until after they are convinced we can deliver on a single product," Rick said. "It could be a lot of wasted effort."

"Penny has a point, though," Ian said. "I'm not sure we could consider it wasted effort if we do a good enough job on the product that they want us to expand to the job. We'll only show them the product campaign, but we'll have everything waiting in the wings for the brand."

IAN AND PENNY sat next to each other at the conference table in his office as they discussed the direction he wanted to take the campaign. He enjoyed meeting with her and was finding excuses for the two of them to have meetings. He'd been focused on his computer with the copy when he looked up a few minutes previously to find her standing in front of the windows. The light silhouetted her and showed the shape of her legs beneath the flowing cotton skirt she wore.

One of the things Ian had done was encourage people to express their own personal style in their workspaces and in their clothing. He'd stressed that they needed to be prepared for professional client meetings, but that normal working days should not require suits and ties. His own suit hung on the back of the office door. He had a fresh white shirt and tie in his desk drawer. But he wore a golf shirt and slacks while he was working. The morale and productivity had gone up in the office since Ian had come in as manager.

Looking at Penny made Ian sigh and she turned to face him.

"Am I distracting you?" she asked.

"Pleasantly. Do you have a minute to go over the concept?" That had started their intense impromptu conversation at the conference table.

"Their original branding worked great for the resorts," Penny said. "It was all about finding the Fountain of Youth. But when they got into physical products, it was harder to stretch the analogy."

"Part of our problem is getting something that bridges the range of products they currently have," Ian said. "And hopefully allowing for an expanded product line. Here's what I've got in mind." He reached for a pad of paper and started to sketch out an idea as he talked. Penny reached over a put a hand on his.

"Don't draw, Ian," she said softly.

Fuck! This was just what he needed. Did she think she had better ideas than his already?

"Talk. Tell me," she continued. "Words are your strength. Images are mine. Let me be the bridge from your words to the images we need."

He looked at her and saw that she wasn't attempting to overrule him, but to become his fingers. He painted with words. She spoke with pictures. He launched into the concept he'd been working on all morning. Occasionally, his fingers itched to draw something, but he was amazed as what he said took shape on the paper under Penny's fingers.

"What about the adult toys aspect?" she asked.

"I think they should expand to have their own retail outlet. Online presence first and then exclusive shops at the resort. They might even expand to a clothing line. How about 'play clothes for adults?' It's the one thing that says more about youth than anything else."

"Play clothes," Penny mused. "How about positioning everything as a playground?"

"I like that. What's in your toybox? Where is your playground? Who is your playmate? What games do you play? What play clothes will you wear? I like it a lot. Can you develop something to go with the idea of an adult playground that is equipped with everything you need to have fun? Fun is the name of the game," Ian said enthusiastically.

"I can develop some rough ideas based on this, but you'll have to provide me with more words for the individual products so I can figure out where on the playground they go." Penny pushed her chair back and stood, leaning forward to kiss Ian on the cheek. "Thank you! This will be so much fun!"

She ran out the door and took up one of the art stations where there was a good supply of markers. Ian watched her go, a little bemused at still feeling the kiss on his cheek.

"I THINK WE can safely say that you've captured what we want for this product line," Ms. Phillips, the CEO of Restore Youth, said. "I love the playfulness. It's something we lack in our previous imagery."

"Thank you," Rick said. "Ian has a team ready to launch production on this with the magazine ads, television, and bill-boards. The proposal you have in front of you contains the details and budget."

"There's one issue before we start production," Ms. Phillips said. "I don't want to be trapped with a product campaign that is a one-off. How soon could I see a brand campaign for the entire Restore Youth line?"

"Tomorrow," Ian said. Rick kicked him.

"Seriously, give us a week," Rick laughed. "Ian's enthusiasm is based on his words. He forgets that people actually have to produce the materials to go with them. Let's set it up for a week from Friday."

"WE'RE SO CLOSE we could have been ready to present tomorrow," Ian said to Rick after the meeting.

"You have a brilliant mind for copy and creativity," Rick said, "but you lack something in the business department. If we came back with the entire brand proposition tomorrow, they'd think it was too easy and not worth what we want to get paid. You and your staff are going to work 'around the clock' for the next week preparing materials and showing our client that we'll move mountains to fulfill our obligations to them. We might even need to extend the deadline by a day or two. And remember, great looking art but absolutely nothing but storyboards. Do not go giving away the idea that we might have film and finished art already."

"That's why I manage creative and you manage the client," Ian laughed. "I'll keep my mouth shut. Our team is so excited about this, though, that I might not be able to keep them from *literally* working around the clock whether they need to or not."

THE CELEBRATION THE following Friday's presentation to the client was epic. Floyd Anderson held an open bar for his employees at O'Malley's. He also saw to it that each employee had a travel voucher and would not be driving.

"Congratulations," he said to Ian. "You've just ensured a happy retirement. This client is going to keep us going for years to come."

"I hope so, but it was really a team effort. We've got great collaborators in our group."

"Speaking of which, are you going to be able to continue managing the group with the amount of writing that will be necessary for this one project?"

"Drake did a great job with the scripts for the ads. He's got a natural talent and is also a good collaborator. I'm going to turn the bulk of the writing over to him and focus on being the creative director and idea generator. Not that I won't be reviewing the writing to make sure it is within our style and voice, but I won't be staying up all night trying to choose the right word," Ian laughed.

"Now if we could just find you a good woman," Floyd laughed. "She'd make sure you didn't stay up all night. Looking for a word."

"I've got a good description of her," Ian said. "Just need to get the picture that matches."

"Hey! Pictures are my specialty," Penny laughed from nearby. She reached in an oversize bag and pulled out a sketchbook and pencil. "Give me the words and let me make a picture out of them."

"You two go have fun," Floyd said as he moved to intercept Rick.

"You want to draw my dream girl? What are you drinking?"

"Macallan 10. Can you afford me?"

"Floyd's footing the bill," Ian laughed. He ordered two drinks and they found a table.

"Well?"

"Really?" She nodded. "Okay then. A picture can only show how she looks, but what's inside is even more important. Yes, she's pretty. She's fit. She's youthful in appearance and action. When she smiles at me, I feel like I'm the most important person in her world. And her body reflects that joy. She's smart. She has a broad view of life with experience to back it up. She can see past the petty issues that crop up and not get distracted from the big things."

It wasn't the same thing he'd written a couple of months ago, but it had the same points. He'd recited them in his head as a nearly daily mantra. While he talked, he dreamed. While he talked, she sketched.

His new version was more than a thousand words. He talked a lot about the way she made him feel and the things they would do together. Occasionally, he mentioned something about how her hand felt in his or the sensation of her lips against his. More and more, he found he was looking at her as he talked, describing Penny's laugh and the way she walked. At last he wound down.

Penny looked at the sketch and then back up at him. She closed the sketchbook and started to put it away.

"Wait! You haven't shown me," he said. "How am I supposed to recognize her?" She hesitated.

"How long ago did you put this dream of yours together?" she asked.

"A few months. While I was on vacation," he responded.

"What would happen if you found you already knew her?"

"I'd be overjoyed. And probably tongue-tied. I don't know that many people unless I work with them."

She sighed, still hesitating with the sketchbook almost in her bag. Finally, she opened it again and looked at the picture and again at Ian. He held out his hand and she gave him the drawing.

"Penny," he said, "this is... Oh, wow. This is you. Are you really the woman of my dreams?"

"How would that make you feel?" she asked grinning at him.

"Like a million bucks."

THEY DIDN'T RUSH to his apartment (or hers) and fall into bed that night. They did, however, have a little too much to drink and shared a deep and sensuous kiss before the cars Floyd had called swept them away to their homes. She'd finally given him the drawing after he'd begged her for it.

"Okay, but no masturbating to it," she laughed. "Tonight."

They talked on the phone the next afternoon and met for a walk along the lake on Sunday. They held hands and talked.

"We can't let dating each other interfere with our workplace," he said. "The last manager had an affair with an artist and it affected his judgment on projects. It was the worst-kept secret in the building. I don't ever want people thinking you are advancing because of our relationship."

"I think we should tell them," Penny suggested. "I don't think anyone would object. Floyd wasn't even objecting. Did you see how he blocked Rick from interrupting us Friday night?"

"The issues of nepotism are always a problem, but when two people click together, it's hard not to want to go further."

"Floyd and I have had to deal with that," she said.

"What? You're involved with Floyd?" Ian said. He stopped dead still and stared at Penny, not sure if he should yell at her or just walk away.

"He's my grandfather," she said simply.

"Your... Oh, my God! That sneaky old bastard."

"He didn't put me up to it," she defended herself—and her grandfather. "But one office secret is all I'm capable of. I'll keep romance out of the office, but I won't keep a secret of the man I love."

"Do you, Penny? Do you know enough about me to say you love me? I've been falling for two months now and resisting because I didn't want to be that kind of a manager."

"Well, I still have to find out if you're as good in bed as you are on paper," she laughed.

THEY DECIDED TO wait until after they had informed the staff they were dating before they rushed to find out.

"Wait! You mean you haven't been dating all this time?" Jill asked. "Damn! I missed my chance."

"Yeah, me too," Dennis sighed as he batted his eyelashes at Ian. Everyone laughed.

"Let me just say I'm a little dense about these things," Ian said.

"Single-minded focus on a project," Lee said. "It's what we love about you."

"Well, if any of you decide at any time that my judgment is being affected by our relationship or that it is interfering with our work, my door stays open. Walk in and tell me. I expect it of you," Ian said.

"That's new," Drake said. "Jack and Georgia always closed and locked the door. We could hear them anyway. Now we get to watch, too."

"There won't be anything to watch in the office," Penny said. "Though, if you haven't taken advantage of his open door to go look out the window, you are really missing something."

IAN AND PENNY dated for two more weeks before they found themselves sharing a drink on Ian's balcony Saturday night.

"Where is the original list of things you described?" Penny asked after she'd kissed him thoroughly.

"Burned," he said. She cocked her head as she looked at him. "After I wrote it, I visualized her—you—and burned the list right here on the grill. I let the wind pick up the ashes and carry them out to find my dream girl and bring her to me."

"And now the girl has materialized on your balcony," she said with another kiss. "Make love to me, Ian. I want you."

He swept her up in his arms and carried her to the bedroom. She was in an outfit he'd found was her favorite style. Mid-calf full cotton skirt in a bright geometric pattern and an embroidered pull-over top with a scoop neckline. It was easy for him to kiss from her cheek down her neck and onto her shoulders. The color of the blouse reflected the indigo of her eyes. She tugged at his shirt and got it off over his head, then removed her own top. She wore no bra and he bent to kiss softly around her breasts before lightly caressing her nipples with his lips.

They lay on the bed exploring each other and kissing, feeling the warmth of skin against skin.

"What do you like, Penny?" he asked.

"Really? You really want to know what I like?"

"Is that so strange?"

"Yeah. Yes, it is. Guys just sort of figure they know what a girl wants. Kiss, suck nipples, lick clit, fuck."

"Excuse my ignorance," he laughed. "Is that what you like?"

"No. I… I like having my shoulders kissed and my back rubbed. I have tight muscles at the base of my neck and want them loosened up so I can turn my head to kiss you. I like to have my buns rubbed and my toes sucked. Then I like to be kissed, sucked, licked, and fucked," she giggled.

"How about we deal with that sore neck first?" he asked. "I don't have any massage oil. Will this lotion be okay?"

"Oh, Ian. Yes. Just your fingers would be okay. Thank you. Oh! That feels so good!" She lay on her stomach and he gently kneaded her sore muscles, liberally sprinkling kisses along her shoulders as he worked. She had incredibly beautiful shoulders. He explored her back, her arms, and her sides. As he moved down her body, he dragged her skirt and panties down so he could pay attention to her bottom. Extrapolating her love of being kissed where he was rubbing, he spread kisses across her cheeks as he smoothed the lotion into her skin. Rather than skipping down to her feet, he kept working down her legs, dragging her clothes the rest of the way off. He worked the lotion into her feet and finally began kissing and sucking her toes. Penny moaned.

"Am I getting all the right spots, love?" he whispered.

"Oh, Ian. So wonderful. I promise I'll ask what you like soon. But now could we move on to kiss, suck, lick, fuck?"

"Your wish is my command," he answered. She turned toward him and tugged at his belt until she managed to unfasten and remove his slacks and shorts. And then they came together in a full-body naked hug for the first time. They started with the kissing part, and Ian did nibble at her breasts a little, but they were both too impatient to bother with licking before fucking. Penny rolled to her back and beckoned Ian between her legs. He was painfully erect and she was extremely wet. They slid together quickly and easily, not stopping until Ian was fully inside her.

"I could get used to this full feeling inside me," Penny said. "I could feel you all the way in. You touched the walls of my vagina all the way to my cervix. I never knew I had so many nerves inside me that had never been stimulated."

"Stimulated is a good word. Everything is being stimulated. The whole length of my cock is being consumed by your pussy. Penny, I won't last long. But I promise I'll make it up to you."

"I'm so close, Ian. Stroke in and out again. I'm on edge. You won't have anything to make up. Yes. Right there." She grabbed his hips and moved them left and right a little, stimulating her clit with his pubic bone. Ian got the message and withdrew to thrust in again and gyrate side to side. "Yes. I can feel it. Almost. One more time, lover. Do it one more time." Ian closed his eyes, panting and trying to focus on her pleasure while his cock was determined to take its own. He thrust one more time and as he moved side to side with his cock fully buried, semen rose through his system and began pumping into her. "Yes!" she screamed. Ian moaned as Penny clamped down around him. His hips jerked involuntarily, trying to drive farther into her depths. He collapsed forward seeking her lips but unable to hold them as he continued to pulse in time with her convulsions.

Aware that he was about to collapse on top of her, he rolled to the side, pulling her with him so they could stay joined as long as possible. She clamped her legs closed to hold him inside. He moaned and at last they found each other's lips again.

"How long do I have to wait before I can tell you how much I love you without having it sound like the sex talking?" he whispered.

"Better not wait. There isn't likely to be enough time between."

"I love you, Penny. You are she for whom I've been searching. I know it's too early to talk about long-term plans and building a life together. I'd like to build a now with you. I love you now and it will always be now."

"I love you, Ian. I've waited all my life for someone who cared enough to ask what I wanted. That what I want is what you have wished for makes my heart sing. I am here now. Love me now."

Devon Layne

ART CAN BE painted, sculpted, perhaps sung, and yes, even written. And in their art, the artists release not only their creativity and their vision, but also their deepest desires. When those desires find the perfect match, a miracle occurs. Galatea emerges from the cold stone and embraces her Pygmalion.

Aphrodite, blessed is love.

www.ingramcontent.com/pod-product-compliance
Lightning Source LLC
Chambersburg PA
CBHW060218180626
46813CB00007B/2873